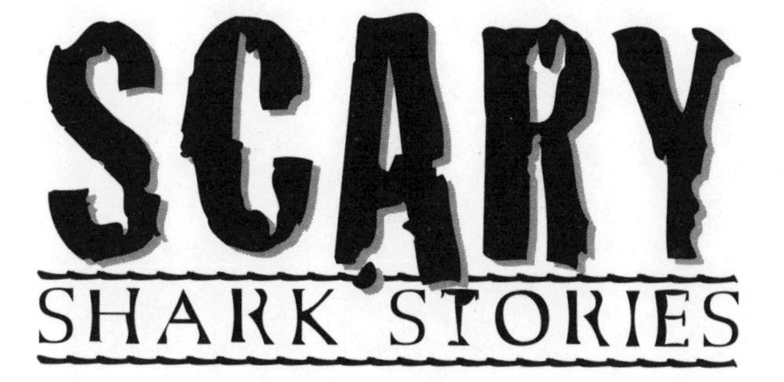
SCARY
SHARK STORIES

by Scott Ingram

interior illustrations by Eric Angeloch

LOWELL HOUSE JUVENILE

LOS ANGELES

CONTEMPORY BOOKS

CHICAGO

Cover illustration by Chris Cocozza

ISBN: 1-56565-614-8
Library of Congress Catalog Card Number is available

Publisher: Jack Artenstein
General Manager, Juvenile Division: Elizabeth Amos
Director of Publishing Services: Rena Copperman
Editor in Chief of Fiction, Juvenile Division: Barbara Schoichet
Managing Editor, Juvenile Division: Lindsey Hay
Art Director: Lisa-Theresa Lenthall

Lowell House books can be purchased at special discounts when ordered in bulk for premiums and special sales. Contact Department JH at the following address:

Lowell House Juvenile
2020 Avenue of the Stars, Suite 300
Los Angeles, CA 90067

Manufactured in the United States of America

10 9 8 7 6 5 4 3 2

Table of Contents

Endless Blue 7

Megamouth 27

Old Whitetip 41

No More Bull 57

Future Shark 77

ENDLESS BLUE

Everywhere he looked, Travis Haley saw sharks. He'd stopped counting at thirty, but there were probably twice as many as that. They were blue sharks, streamlined creatures with long, pointed snouts and double rows of fin-shaped teeth angling back in their jaws.

Travis knew sharks, and since blues were the most common ocean sharks off the Southern California coast, he'd seen them before. Most of these looked to be at least six feet long, but it was hard to tell exactly. The water was nearly a thousand feet deep, and looking down off the stern of the boat, it was hard for Travis to judge their size against the bottomless blue background.

It was the first day that fourteen-year-old Travis had felt well enough to be on his feet. He hadn't expected to get seasick. In fact, he'd never been sick on a boat before—then again, he'd never been this far out before, either. Seventy-five miles off the coast of Southern California was quite a distance, and as soon as the *Tropic Breeze* had left sight of land two days earlier, the boat's rolling motion had put Travis in a constant battle with nausea.

But luckily for Travis, the *Tropic Breeze* was nearly seventy feet long, with the bridge rising ten feet over the deck. That meant that it was large enough not to pitch back and forth too much. Still, the gentle lifting and falling in the wide-open Pacific surf had kept Travis from eating anything solid since they'd left port. Today he'd finally been able to have some orange juice and a little cereal.

Travis's big problem was that he had a job to do, and for the past two days all he'd done was lie in his bunk, groaning. Now, feeling more like the young sailor he was, Travis had his wet suit and weight belt on, ready to dive, ready to get to work.

"You're not so green this morning, bud," Marcus Haley said, throwing his arm over his son's shoulder. Travis looked up at his father. He was only a few inches shorter than his dad, who was a little under six feet. Both were thin, with crew-cut brown hair. They also had the same green eyes and wide, square front teeth.

"Yeah, I'm back from the dead," Travis said, smiling.

"Are you ready to back me up, then?" his dad asked eagerly. "Without a safety diver, I haven't been able to do any shooting." He paused for a moment and looked gravely at his son. "Now listen, Travis, if you can't dive today, I'll wear the metal shark suit."

"I *think* I'm okay to dive," Travis said hesitantly.

"Well, are you backing me up or not?" His dad stood there, his hands on his hips. "You can't just *think* you're ready to go under; you have to *know* you're ready."

Travis heard the edge in his father's voice and knew that he had to come up with an answer. The metal shark suit made it almost impossible to move quickly enough to photograph undersea creatures, and since Marcus Haley was one of the best-known underwater photographers in the world, he had to shoot while the shooting was good—even if it meant wearing his bulky diving gear.

Travis felt just awful. His dad had brought him on this week-long photo shoot—an assignment for *Ocean Adventures* magazine—only because the job had a tight deadline and he didn't have time to hire his usual back-up divers. It was supposed to be Travis's job to keep an eye out for attacking sharks while his dad snapped the incredible close-up shots that had made him world famous. Now, because of Travis's stupid bout of green gills, his father's tight schedule was threatened.

Seeing his father waiting for a response, Travis looked away. He had no idea what to do. He'd jumped at the chance to spend time with his dad, and before he'd gotten seasick he was certain that he could do a good job as a shark lookout. After all, Travis had been diving almost every day since sixth grade, and had logged hundreds of hours exploring the reefs in the San Diego Underwater Park. He was a very good diver—just like his dad—so there was no reason to lose his confidence now.

But the deepest water he'd ever dived in was only thirty feet. This was his first chance to dive in water so deep there would be nothing but blue emptiness above and below him. It was also the first time he and his dad would be diving together since his parents had divorced and Travis had gone to live with his mother.

"Come on, son," his father said impatiently. "Are you going with me or not?"

Travis's stomach began to churn. Was he seasick again . . . or just afraid? His dad was a hard-driving man, a no-nonsense perfectionist. His work was his life, and he didn't have time for wishy-washiness. When Marcus Haley was given an assignment, he did it. When he was asked to travel to the ends of the earth for a particular shot, he went. In fact, Travis hardly remembered his dad ever being around much, and he was pretty sure that all his father's globe-trotting had been part of the reason for the divorce. Even as a kid Travis had understood the unspoken messages in slammed doors, angry stares, and forced smiles when his father had returned after months of being away.

Now an old anger rose up in Travis, and he was about to tell his father that he could just go dive by himself—like he always did—but then a whirring sound of a mechanical pulley caught Travis's attention. He looked over his father's shoulder to the port side of the boat. A steel shark cage was hanging over the water on a boom. The cage looked like a portable jail cell about the size of a small elevator, with a break in the bars at eye level for placing a camera.

Inside the bars was Deborah Dove, a famous deep-sea photographer. She was shooting footage for *Fintastic Creatures,* a documentary she was doing for the Science Channel. The cage would be her only protection from a shark attack and was to take the place of a backup diver.

Travis knew that Deborah Dove was another reason why his father had been on edge for the past two days. When they'd arrived at the dock, he and his father had discovered that Jack Morris, captain of the *Tropic Breeze,* had made a scheduling mistake, accidentally chartering his boat out to *two* photography groups. Travis and his dad made up one party, and his dad's photojournalist rival, Deborah Dove, along with her fourteen-year-old daughter, Ashley, made up the other.

"Hi, Travis!" Ms. Dove waved to him from inside the cage. "Feeling better?"

"Yes, thank you!" Travis called, waving back. "Plenty of sharks around today. I've already spotted over two dozen!" Unlike his dad, Travis was easygoing, a talker who'd strike up a conversation with just about anybody.

"Well, there should be a lot of action," Ms. Dove said in her brisk, businesslike tone. "The crew has been throwing chopped fish overboard since dawn."

She made a few last-minute adjustments to her camera, then nodded to the deckhands, who began to lower the cage. Travis watched in awe as the sharks instantly swirled around the cage the moment it hit the water. Then he saw the shadow of someone on the other side of the boat. It was Ashley Dove, who had appeared on deck just as her mother's cage sank into the bright water.

One of the prettiest girls Travis had ever seen, Ashley had raven-black hair in a braid that fell to the middle of her back, and eyes as blue as the ocean. She waved to her mother, who was too busy to wave back. Then Ashley saw Travis and waved to him.

"Hey, Trav! Guess you're feeling okay, huh?" Ashley said in her usual perky voice. "Hope you don't hurl into your air hose!" She burst out laughing.

Travis had to laugh, too. If it hadn't been for Ashley, the last two days would have been ten times worse. She'd brought him ginger ale and had let him use her Walkman. They'd talked about sharks a lot, too—at least

Ashley had talked—and Travis found out that she knew more about the fascinating creatures than any diver he'd ever met.

"Hey, Ash," Travis called. "If I *do* get sick, are you gonna be there to—"

"Travis! Are you gonna talk all day?" his father asked sharply. "The water may not stay clear too long for shooting. Look," he said, pointing to the water, "the fish scraps are already making it murky. Now, are you going with me or not?"

All he thinks about are his precious photos, Travis thought, embarrassed by the way his father talked to him in front of Ashley. *He could care less about me!*

"All right, I'm coming," he called with the same edge to his voice his father had just used. He put on his tanks and flippers and made his way clumsily over the stern to the low diving platform that hung a few feet over the water.

"We shouldn't have any trouble if we stay up current from this bloody chum," his dad said, referring to the chopped fish that was used to attract the sharks. "But take the shark club anyway." And with that, he put on his face mask and climbed down to the platform with his camera.

Travis hooked a thick metal rod to his weight belt and looked into the water. He hoped he wouldn't have to smash any sharks with it. Once before, when diving off San Diego with a couple of guys from his scuba club, Travis had clobbered a gray reef shark that had come too near. The shark had come up fast, and luckily had backed off that time, but Travis was never quite sure if any metal rod could be much defense if a shark *really* wanted to get at someone.

Travis had learned from his father that usually sharks came close only out of curiosity. In fact, most experienced divers agreed that blue sharks—the kind swirling in the water now—were pussycats compared to big ocean sharks like tigers or great whites. Still, every time he looked into the water and saw a wriggling mass of dark-blue shapes, Travis couldn't help but feel a knot tie in his stomach. He'd never dived into a crowd of excited sharks feeding on chum before, and he didn't exactly relish the idea.

But not wanting to look like a coward in front of his father or Ashley, Travis controlled his trembling hands and held his mask tightly over his face. Then he sat next to his father on the platform, ready to roll into the water.

At the last instant, his dad looked down and studied the swarm of sharks. Travis could tell he was thinking about something. *Great, if Mr. Nerves-of-Steel is having second thoughts, we're really in trouble,* Travis thought.

Then his father turned around and grabbed another rod, about the size of a small baseball bat. At the end was what looked like a firecracker. "Take this bang stick, too," he said, looking at Travis gravely. "If the club won't keep them away from me, don't hesitate to use it. When you whack one on the nose, the shell will go off." He paused, making sure he had his son's full attention. "Remember, Travis, I've got two days of shooting to make up. I'm gonna be too busy to pay attention to anything but my light meter and viewfinder. Be sharp down there, okay?"

Travis nodded, and upon his father's thumbs-up, the two rolled into the water simultaneously and sank into the blue void.

Instantly Travis felt more like an astronaut on a space walk than a scuba diver, and his excitement about the underwater world around him made him forget about his queasy stomach. With his father in the lead, they dove to thirty feet, surrounded in every direction by endless blue that was broken only by the silhouette of the boat's hull above . . . and the glint of Deborah Dove's shark cage suspended in watery space about twenty yards away.

Under the boat, thick clusters of sharks swarmed like flies—six-foot flies with very sharp teeth. Travis moved into position near his father, who was busy snapping photos. Already sharks had begun to bump them, but Travis wasn't too scared. He could see that although most of the beasts were well over six feet, none of them had their mouths open. It was more like they were just giving him nosey shoves, which were easy to fend off. And fend off he did. He hit, pushed, and prodded the big fish to force them away, but they kept coming back toward him with seemingly endless curiosity.

Each time the rough-skinned creatures brushed past his wet suit, Travis felt his stomach flip as their dead black eyes stared at him. Then he'd poke the creatures with the shark club on their sensitive snouts, sending them scurrying like huge gray mice into the blue, only to return for yet another shove.

There were so many sharks that Travis had his hands full keeping the nosey creatures from disturbing his father, who signaled that he was going deeper. Marcus Haley was famous for his underwater-to-surface shots, in which he used the sunlight to frame a shark's silhouette, and Travis suspected that his father was going after the perfect cover photo for his current assignment.

Several big blues were following his father now, nudging the relentless photographer and keeping him from getting a steady picture. Travis could see that his father was becoming frustrated. He kept pointing to sharks that were too close and gesturing for Travis to keep them away.

I'm doing my best! Travis thought angrily as he felt his arms tire from punching the monsters. *Can't he see that?*

Suddenly Travis's eyes were drawn to motion and sound that wasn't around his father but instead was over by Deborah Dove's shark cage. Through the blue haze of water he saw a cloud of air bubbles and *two* shapes in the cage—and one of them wasn't human.

For a moment Travis forgot about his father and swam toward Ms. Dove, slowly at first, and then with a burst of speed when he realized what was happening. A small blue shark, no more than four feet long, had gotten through the bars. When the creature realized that it might be cornered, it had panicked and gone after Ms. Dove!

As he drew closer, Travis saw that the shark had its jaws locked on the woman's forearm. She was pounding on the fish, but it wasn't letting go. Instead, it tugged on her arm like a small dog with a pant leg in its teeth.

Then Travis started to panic, too. As he looked into the cage, now only a few feet away, he saw a cloud of blood fanning out among the rising air bubbles . . . and he could hear Ms. Dove's muted screams! He had to help her. But what could he do? He knew he couldn't squeeze into the cage's opening. He couldn't—

Suddenly Travis got an idea. He quickly reached through the bars and grabbed the shark's tail. Then, pulling with all his strength, he yanked the startled shark away from the bleeding woman's arm.

As the fish crashed blindly into the steel bars, searching for a way out, Travis froze. Now what? The shark could strike Ms. Dove again at any second!

Then he remembered the bang stick his father had given him. Without hesitating another second, Travis grabbed it from his belt, and in one rapid striking motion, he thrust it through the bar, hitting the beast just below its bottom jaw.

PHOOOOMP! The muffled blast of the shell knocked Travis back. He looked into the cage. The blast had blown the shark to ribbons. Its shattered half-body lay at the bottom of the cage, spewing blood.

But that wasn't the worst of it. Now excited sharks began to appear from every direction out of the blue curtain of ocean, bumping against the cage. In an effort to help Ms. Dove, Travis had started a feeding frenzy!

Ms. Dove was slumped against the back of the cage, her left hand clamped tightly over her right forearm. Then, at last, Travis saw the cage rise. Somehow she had managed to alert the crew above to bring her up.

As Travis moved away from the sharks trailing the cage, he had an uncomfortable feeling that his father might be upset. But as he turned to swim back, Travis saw that his father was only a few feet away. He'd been snapping pictures of the whole horrific event—snapping pictures . . . but not helping.

Now it was Deborah Dove's turn to lose a few days of shooting. The bite had sliced open the thick flesh on her upper forearm near the elbow, and the shark's jagged teeth had nearly cut through to the bone.

Luckily the *Tropic Breeze* had recently been outfitted with the newest communications equipment, including a cellular phone, a modem, a fax, and a satellite dish for navigation and for sending out locator signals. Captain Morris had immediately notified the coast guard, and a helicopter with medics had arrived on the scene less than an hour after the attack.

Ms. Dove's wound took more than eighty stitches. The medics had wanted to airlift her back to a hospital so a surgeon could look at the jagged cut, but the fearless photojournalist had steadfastly refused.

"Absolutely not!" she'd said. "As long as I can still hold a camera, I'm staying right here."

No amount of reasoning by the medics or pleading from Ashley could shake her. All she'd asked for were some pain pills. Then she'd retreated to her room, promising to wait a few days before she insisted on going out shooting again.

It was the second night after the accident, and Travis still couldn't believe that his father had done nothing to help Ms. Dove. Now, as he sat next to Ashley near the stern and the two gazed at stars splashed across the sky like paint drops flicked from a giant brush, he wanted to talk about the whole thing. But all he could do was ask, "How's your mom doing?"

"Okay, I guess," Ashley said wearily. "As okay as she can be after being a shark snack." She paused and looked into Travis's eyes. "I'm worried, Travis. My mom says she's going to start filming again tomorrow."

"Really?" Travis said in a surprised tone. "You mean she wants to go back down with all those sharks?"

Travis wasn't talking about just blue sharks, either. In the past two days, larger sharks had begun clustering around the boat—huge sharks as big as trailer trucks on the highway. He'd seen hammerheads, makos, blacktips, and that afternoon, a tiger shark that he'd guessed was approximately fifteen feet long. Even after the crew stopped throwing out fish scraps, the sharks remained in the area, their dark shapes swirling around the boat like iron filings attracted to a magnet.

"Travis, my mother has a ton of money invested in this documentary. She has to finish it by the deadline to make any profit," Ashley explained. "She's also one of the most competitive people in the universe."

"Competitive?" Travis asked. "What does that have to do with anything?"

"It has to do with your father," Ashley replied. "He's the big photo hotshot, but my mother thinks she's as good with film as he is with still photography. She's not going to give up the best shark shooting she's ever seen—*especially* with your father around."

"There are some incredible shots to be had down there," Travis had to admit. "I've never seen so many different kinds of sharks in one place."

"Me either," Marcus Haley said, surprising the two teenagers as he came out on deck. "I've never been out at a better location."

"Really?" Travis asked, forgetting for a moment how angry he still was at his dad. He couldn't help being impressed with his father's comment. If *he'd* never seen so many sharks, that meant they were really swarming.

"Yup," his dad said. "I just developed another roll. Want to see what I've got?"

"Sure!" Travis and Ashley said in unison.

But just then a beep from a cellular ship-to-shore phone interrupted their plans. Mr. Haley shrugged and pulled a portable receiver from a pack at his waist and dialed several numbers to open a channel.

As his father dialed, Travis looked over the side and saw several dorsal fins circling close to the boat. He also heard the raspy sound of sandpaperlike skin scraping against the hull. The monsters were down there, all right.

"Yes, this is Marcus Haley," his dad was saying softly into the phone, turning away from the teenagers. "Right, the shark photographer. I called the *Weekly Examiner* because I have some photos I think you might like."

Ashley looked at Travis and raised her eyebrows. The *Weekly Examiner* printed two-headed-alien-baby stories. Travis looked back and shrugged.

"It's of a shark attack," Mr. Haley said, unaware that his voice was carrying through the still night air. "Only a small shark, but there's a whole bunch of blood. Then the shark gets blown to bits and there's a huge feeding frenzy. Pretty nasty." He chuckled. "I got the cut on the diver, too—close up."

Travis looked sheepishly at Ashley. His father was selling pictures of the attack on her mother, an attack he could have at least tried to stop but instead hadn't lifted a finger!

"Great!" Mr. Haley said. "I'll fax some shots tonight. If you like them, I'll send the glossies and the negatives." He paused. "Permission? Um . . . yeah, sure. My son was one diver. The other . . . well, she won't be a problem."

"I can't believe it," Ashley whispered, shaking her head. "If my mother finds out, she'll go bananas. No way she'd let him use shots of her like that."

"Should I say something?" Travis asked. He knew his father was doing something that wasn't quite right.

But he didn't want to stick his nose where it didn't belong, either.

Ashley sighed. "I guess not. They're adults. Let them work out their own hassles. As far as I'm concerned, I didn't hear a thing." She yawned. "I'm gonna turn in. I'll look at your father's pictures another time."

"See you tomorrow," Travis said, avoiding Ashley's gaze. He couldn't help feeling embarrassed, and as soon as his father ended the call, Travis started back to his bunk.

"Where's Ashley?" Mr. Haley asked. "And where are you going? I thought you two wanted to see the shots I just developed."

"She was tired," Travis said, coldly walking past his father. "And so am I."

"But what about the pictures, Trav?" his dad asked. "Don't you want to see 'em?"

"Maybe tomorrow," Travis grunted. And with that he left his father alone on the deck, looking over the side at the dorsal fins circling and circling and circling.

The next morning, Ms. Dove was on deck when Travis came out in his wet suit. She stood next to Ashley and looked over the side at the clustering of sharks below, her heavily bandaged arm bulging through her tight diving suit. Travis walked over and stood beside the two as they stared down into the water.

"Are you diving today, Ms. Dove?" he asked, after nodding hello.

"I have my wet suit on, don't I?" Ms. Dove said with tension in her voice.

"Mom, Travis was only asking because of all the sharks," Ashley said, rolling her eyes as she looked at Travis. "They've been acting really strange."

"I'm sorry, Travis," Ms. Dove said icily. "I've missed two days of shooting. Today is my last chance. I guess I'm a little edgy."

"Maybe you should take this shark club down in the cage with you," Travis suggested, picking up the thick pole.

"I think I'll be needing that, Travis," his dad said, suddenly appearing on deck and taking the club.

Travis turned toward his father and was surprised to see that he was wearing the metal suit.

"I'm only going down alone for a few minutes, Trav," he said. "No need for you to come with me. Besides, the sharks seem very excited. A couple of them rammed into the boat a while ago. I've never seen anything like it so I'm not taking any chances. The suit—and this club—will give me enough protection."

Ms. Dove turned away from Travis and Mr. Haley. She looked at her daughter, then at her camera, tanks, and other gear. "Give me a hand, will you, Ashley? My arm is still kind of sore."

Since his father didn't need help, Travis moved to help Ashley, but Ms. Dove held up her hand. "Look, Travis, I appreciate your help. And even though I haven't said anything, I'm grateful for what you did the other day. But Ashley and I can manage by ourselves—we're used to it."

"Whatever," Travis said, trying to hide the painful feelings that flooded through him.

Ashley rolled her eyes at Travis again as she lifted the heavy air tank onto her mother's back and mouthed

"I'm sorry." Then both of them watched as Ms. Dove climbed into the small cage and signaled to go down.

The cage sank beneath the waves in minutes, and dark shapes immediately began to circle the metal bars. Then, when Mr. Haley dove from the stern, some of the creatures moved in his direction as if deciding he looked more tasty. Trying to appear calm, Travis and Ashley stood side by side, looking at their parents.

"Maybe they won't stay down long," Ashley said. "Once my mother hears some shark teeth clang off that metal, she'll—"

But Ashley stopped in midsentence, her eyes wide with fear. "Oh, no! I just figured it out!"

"What? Figured out what?" Travis asked, feeling panic rise within him.

"The sharks. Why they're swarming around the boat!" she said. "It's their ampullae!"

Travis frowned. "Their what?" he asked. "What are *am-pew-lay?*"

Ashley's voice quivered as she explained the term. "All sharks have something like a sixth sense—it helps them to navigate."

"Like a satellite dish," Travis said, glancing up at the large white revolving disk on the bridge.

"Right. On sharks they're called the Ampullae of Lorenzini," Ashley said. "I read about it in this cool encyclopedia on sharks. Anyway, Lorenzini was some kind of scientist, and he discovered ampullae. They're like jelly-filled tubes running along a shark's nose and around its head."

"I must be dense, Ash. I'm not understanding what you're getting at," Travis said, frowning. "What does that have to do with how strange the sharks are acting?"

"You know how ever since we left port, Captain Morris has been bragging about all the new electronic equipment he just had installed?" Ashley asked.

"Yeah . . . hey, wait a minute!" Travis said, slowly beginning to follow Ashley's explanation. "The other night when my father had the cellular phone on deck, sharks started bumping against the boat!"

"That's right," Ashley said. "I think whoever installed the new electronic equipment might have goofed, and somehow the boat may be giving off an electric current underwater that's confusing the sharks!"

"Well, that makes sense, Ash," Travis said, truly impressed. "But why are you so worried?"

"Travis . . . sharks have ampullae for one other thing besides navigation," Ashley said, taking a deep breath. "Ampullae help sharks find their prey. They can detect incredibly small electrical fields."

"So *that's* why they swarmed around the metal parts of the boat *and* around the cage. It's also why they bumped into us—our tanks are *metal*!" Travis's heart flopped and his eyes opened wide. "My father—he's in his *metal* shark suit!"

Before anyone could stop him, Travis strapped on a tank and a weight belt. Then he grabbed a bang stick and tumbled into the blue void. The water was thick with sharks, swimming in a strange ballet beneath the boat and around Ms. Dove's shark cage. At first Travis could not locate his father. Then he saw the glimmer of the metal suit about thirty yards away.

His camera hanging from a strap around his chest, Mr. Haley had become sort of a shark magnet. He was swinging the shark club with both hands—like a batter fighting off fast pitches from a ball machine—but some of the sharks were already tugging at his legs and taking nips at his body. The hard metal shell was fending them off . . . but for how long?

Travis sucked in huge lungfuls of air as he swam to help his father. He wasn't exactly sure what he was going to do, but he figured that a bang stick could kill at least one shark and maybe clear an escape path to the surface for his dad.

But Travis didn't see the monstrous shape rising up from the bottomless blue depths until it was too late. His dad *never* saw it. The only indication that he was aware of seeing anything was the big burst of air bubbles that carried his muffled scream to the surface as his lower body vanished between a terrible set of dagger-toothed jaws. It was clearly the biggest shark Travis had ever seen—more than twenty feet long—and its gray back and white belly was all the evidence Travis needed to know that he was looking at a great white.

Close enough to see the wide-eyed terror in his father's face, Travis screamed along with him as the creature crushed his father's body right through the tight metal suit. Then, as the monster dove straight down, disappearing into the blue with the limp shiny shape clamped between its teeth, Travis heard the *crump* of his father's exploding air tanks and knew there would be no body to find. What was left would sink to the bottom in the heavy suit.

Frozen in horror, Travis floated as sharks bumped his tanks. His father was dead, but his mind still could not accept what his eyes had just seen. Slowly, as everything began to register, he turned back in the direction of the boat. In the distance, he saw the shark cage rising up toward the surface.

"Travis! Travis!" Ashley stood on the diving platform. "Your father—" But then she stopped and looked into Travis's eyes. All she could do was stand there silently as he climbed clumsily from the water, removed his tank, and slumped to the platform.

It was only after somebody lifted him onto the deck that Travis let go of his anguished sobs. He couldn't believe what had just happened, but he *really* couldn't fathom what he was hearing now. It was the static beep and squawk of the ship-to-shore phone, and Ms. Dove with a receiver in her hand, talking into it.

"Hello, *Eyewitness News*?" she was saying, unaware that anyone was listening. "My name is Deborah Dove. I've just filmed the most incredible footage of a shark attack that you'll ever see!"

MEGAMOUTH

The weathered, dark-green wooden boat with Santa Maria *boldly painted on the side is barely large enough to hold four men and two fishing nets as it sets off in the predawn darkness. Swells splash the men as the engine chugs through the inky night, taking them far from their huts and their sleeping families back on the shore.*

Clouds move away, and moonlight dances on the waves as the nets are unfolded and dropped over the side. The thick cords sink into the depths and the men wait for the haul, hoping that this catch will allow them to feed their families for at least another week.

Waves churn and toss the boat back and forth. The men are surprised, since the night air is calm and the sea should be flat. Suddenly they see what looks like an island surface next to them—only the "island" has a monstrous fin rising up into the night over their heads.

"It has returned!" an old fisherman shouts.

Then the moonlight vanishes and the men see only a moving mass of gristle and teeth. It takes half the boat into its mouth and cracks the wooden hull like a peanut shell.

Throat-ripping screams split the night. Jagged teeth as large as shovel blades tear flesh and snap bones. Rivers of blood gush into the blue water, and the last thing the men see is each other's bodies disappearing into the black cave that is the monster's huge mouth. Then the living island submerges, leaving only splinters of the boat, fragments of what once were humans, and empty nets drifting on the current.

"Papa! Mama!" Ruben Ortiz cried. "Help! Help!"

The light snapped on and Ruben's parents ran to their son's bedside. He sat upright, his eyes half-open, his arms clawing out as if trying to escape.

"Wake up, Ruben!" his mother shouted. "It's only a bad dream!"

"Yes, son. You're having a nightmare," his father said, rubbing the thirteen-year-old's thin shoulders.

Ruben shook his head. "No, no, it was real! A real shark, and it swallowed a fishing boat, just like the boats on Isla Perdido."

"But, Ruben, we haven't even been to the island yet," his father insisted. "How can you dream of a place you have seen only in pictures?"

"Your papa is right," Ruben's mother said as she stroked her son's hair, thick and coal black like her own. "Besides, no shark—not even a great white—could swallow a fishing boat whole."

Ruben squinted in the harsh light of the uncovered bulb hanging from the ceiling. The hotel in this seaport village in Costa Rica didn't offer anything close to the luxury Ruben was used to back in Mexico City.

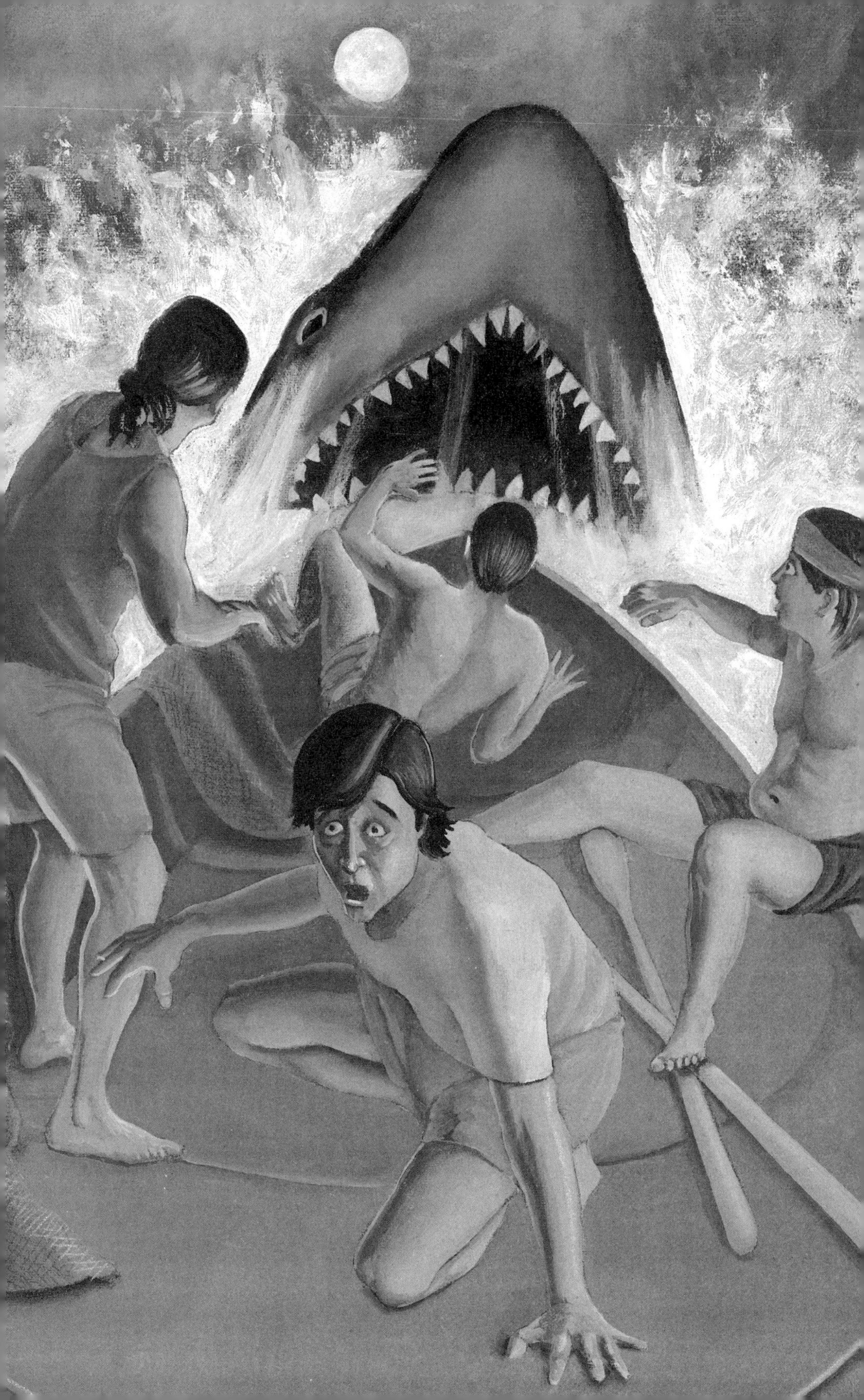

His parents, Dr. Reynaldo Ortiz and Dr. Alma Ortiz—both world-famous paleontologists at the University of Mexico—had spent almost their whole careers traveling the world searching for fossil remains of prehistoric creatures. Hard workers who were well-compensated for the amazing finds they shared with museums all over the world, the Ortizes now lived in a palatial home high in the hills overlooking Mexico City.

Calming down, Ruben thought of his lavish home and wished he could be there now, in his own bed. Instead, he was a thousand miles southeast of his home, waiting with his parents to hitch a ride on a ship that would take them to an island forty miles out in the middle of the Pacific Ocean. The island was called *Isla Perdido*—Lost Island—and it was a rocky, tear-shaped spot of land formed around an extinct volcano. The only inhabitants were several dozen families who had lived there in a fishing village for generations.

The Ortizes learned that the island got its name because of its remote location and because of the eerie legends that surrounded it—legends of fishing boats vanishing and of men sailing away from home, never to return. The legends also told of wood splinters, bone fragments, and huge triangular teeth washing up on the rocky shores.

Ruben's parents decided to explore Isla Perdido because of a discovery they had made several months earlier. They had been in Costa Rica digging for buried fossils near the coast when one day Alma Ortiz had noticed a farmer at work in his field near the dig.

The old man had been clearing weeds between rows of corn that grew in the rich, coffee-colored soil when his hoe had caught Alma's eye. Its blade was a triangular shape and looked as if it were made of dark bone. At first, Dr. Ortiz had thought it might be a fossil from the area. She immediately offered to buy it from the farmer for twenty pesos, and the man had gladly sold the tool. The meager sum, after all, was more than he would earn in a month, and as he'd explained to Dr. Ortiz, he could always trade cornmeal to the fishermen from Isla Perdido for another hoe blade.

Dr. Ortiz had quickly returned to the campsite to show the triangular blade to her husband, who had been marking and cataloging samples from the dig. They examined the triangular blade closely under a magnifying glass.

"It looks like a fossilized tooth, Alma," Reynaldo Ortiz had told his wife. "It may be from the *Carcharodon megalodon.* I didn't think fossils of the Miocene great white sharks could be found in Central America, but this tooth has the same shape, and the same jagged edges, as other specimens I've seen."

"I know," Alma had said, stretching a tape measure against one long side of the blade. "But this tooth is eight inches long."

"That's what makes me curious," Reynaldo had replied, scratching his head. "An eight-inch tooth would have to come from a shark at least eighty feet long!"

"So, what you're saying is that if this *is* a fossil tooth from *Carcharodon megalodon,* its jaws would hold half a dozen humans!" Alma had exclaimed.

"Impossible," Reynaldo had muttered, scraping soil away from the tooth and peering at its surface. Then, suddenly, he'd looked up and stared at his wife. "We must go to Isla Perdido. This is either a hoax or the greatest discovery of our careers!"

"But we still have work to do digging fossils at this site," Alma had reminded her husband. "'Can't this wait until we've—"

"No!" he'd nearly shouted with excitement. "Don't you realize how much more important this find is? This tooth comes from a *living* creature!"

And so now here they were—Alma and Reynaldo Ortiz, with their son, Ruben—sitting on a supply boat as it crashed through heavy seas on a forty-mile journey from the mainland of Costa Rica to Isla Perdido. Ruben stood at the rail, staring down into the blue water. At his side were the family's travel bags and scuba equipment. All were good divers, having spent many a vacation exploring the shallow waters near Acapulco, Hawaii, and the Bahamas. But even though this trip came when school was out, Ruben didn't consider it a vacation. So far, with all the bad dreams he'd been having, he could only view their journey as a nightmare.

In fact, Ruben could not get the terrible images out of his head. It had been almost as though he, too, had been swallowed by the enormous finned creature as it gobbled down the luckless fishermen each night in his dreams.

Anxious about his nightmares, Ruben's parents were even more concerned about the Miocene great white they were tracking. Although they weren't having nightmares about the beast like Ruben was, ever since they had returned from the dig in Costa Rica, all they could talk about was the gigantic tooth and the monster shark from which it came.

Trying to understand why his mother and father were so preoccupied with this particular expedition—after all, dinosaur fossils were nothing new to them—Ruben began reading research articles he'd found piled on their desks about *Carcharodon megalodon*. If he and his parents were going to this island in the middle of nowhere based on the discovery of this one particular shark fossil, Ruben wanted to know all he could about it.

But Ruben hardly had to read more than a single article before he figured out why his parents' mission was so important. Up until their find, fossil remains of the prehistoric great white shark showed that the beast grew to a length of forty feet—big enough to swallow a horse. But this prehistoric creature they were seeking off the waters of Isla Perdido was possibly *twice* that big—and capable of swallowing a *whale*!

Megamouth—that's what Ruben had named the gigantic shark when he'd heard his parents describing the monster to their disbelieving friends at a going-away party. "The tooth is *real*, not a fossil!" his father had told a fellow paleontologist with boyish excitement. "Do you understand what that means?"

When Ruben had overheard the conversation, he knew what his father was getting at. The monster could be out there somewhere . . . and it could be *alive*! His imagination running wild, Ruben's terrible dreams had begun that very same night. And each time they got worse and worse until now, in the latest dream, the monster shark was swallowing whole ships—ships like the one he was on that very moment.

Sorry that he'd begged his parents to let him come on the trip, Ruben now wished more than anything that he was relaxing by their pool back in Mexico City. But it had sounded like such an adventure—and his dreams, after all, weren't real . . . were they?

Three short blasts from the horn on the ship's bridge signaled that the island was near. Instantly Ruben's heart began beating rapidly. He saw children running along a pier that extended a hundred feet out into the water. They were all smiling and waving excitedly. The ship docked there only once a week, carrying food, medicine, mail, and other supplies for the tiny island so far from civilization.

The engine growled as the ship's captain reversed the propeller blades to slow down the heavily loaded craft. Ruben looked at the small fishing boats tied along the wooden pier and the fishing nets hung out on stakes to dry. Suddenly his blood ran cold, and he leaned forward, staring wide-eyed.

"What is it, son?" his father asked, coming up on deck and seeing Ruben's face turn pale with fear.

"That—that boat, Papa," Ruben stammered. "The one being pulled up on the beach by those four men—"

"Yes, Ruben, I see the boat," his father replied. "What about it?"

"It—it's dark green, Papa," Ruben said, his voice quivering. "It's the boat from my dream!"

Orange-and-yellow sunlight of late afternoon dances off white-capped waves. A sleek twenty-five-foot boat powered by a throbbing engine skips over the water like a stone. A stern-faced man wearing aviator glasses and a starched uniform steers the craft while a dark-haired woman scans the horizon with binoculars.

The man checks his instrument panel and tells the woman they are about five miles west of the village. He stops and drops anchor. The boat bounces like a cork as the man stands to help the woman put on her scuba tanks.

Suddenly an immense black shadow darkens the aquamarine water beneath the boat. The rocking becomes more violent, and the craft sways crazily from side to side. Before they can steady themselves, the boat capsizes and the man and the woman are flung overboard.

The shadow rises toward the helpless people as they fight to stay afloat in the rolling waves. There is a sucking sound as water rushes into an opening. It is the creature's mouth, and the man and woman are being drawn into it as though caught in a whirlpool. Their efforts to escape are futile, and death comes quickly as jagged triangular teeth do their work. Instantly the watery cavern that is the shark's jaws is filled with warm fountains of blood.

Ruben awoke covered with sweat. He was in the small hut he and his parents had been given by the villagers to use as sleeping quarters. The sun was already high in the sky. He slept late after a disturbing night. Again, he had dreamed of the monster.

As he lay in bed trying to get up, Ruben suddenly became aware of the sound of crying and wailing. He threw off the mosquito net that covered him and sat up. From the window over the bed he could see the shore, and there, on the pier, he saw several women surrounded by small children. All were sobbing and shaking their heads. Then Ruben saw that his parents were there! Jumping out of bed, he quickly dressed and ran to the dock.

When he got to the scene, a crowd had gathered. Picking up bits of frantic conversation, Ruben came to understand that a fishing boat had gone out before dawn and had not returned. Other fishermen who had left at the same time had returned hours ago with an extra net. They'd found it floating on the waves about five miles west, where the water was no more than fifty feet deep because of a volcanic ridge that had formed below the surface. Millions of fish fed there, but most fishermen stayed away from the area because of all the frightening legends surrounding it.

Several villagers were examining the recovered net, which had been torn into several pieces and had bits of clothing, along with what appeared to be human flesh, trapped in the cord. The villagers were also passing around an object and nodding sadly. The object was a large triangular white tooth.

Ruben pushed closer to his parents at the center of the group. He saw his father talking to some older men, asking questions about other disappearances in the past. Looking worried, Ruben's mother stood off to the side, shaking her head.

Ruben walked over to his mother and gently tapped her on the shoulder. "Did the missing boat have a name, Mama?" he asked.

"The *Santa Maria*," she said absentmindedly, looking out to sea. "It was the green boat that you and your papa were pointing to yesterday when we docked."

Ruben tried to calm his hammering heart. "H-how many men are missing, Mama?" he stammered.

"Four," his mother answered. "I just made a call to the coastal patrol on the shortwave radio. They have a large ship in the area and will launch a search boat at once."

"A search boat?" Ruben asked. "Don't most of those large boats have helicopters on them? It would make searching much faster."

"The captain said the only helicopter is on a mission," his mother replied. "But he said that the search boat is very fast. It can easily cover a great expanse of ocean in a short time."

Ruben could not ignore the horrible fear that was gnawing at him. Then he heard the throbbing sound of a powerful engine in the distance and soon saw a sleek twenty-five-foot boat speeding into view. As it came nearer, skipping over the waves, Ruben saw that a stern-faced man wearing aviator glasses was at the wheel. Then he felt his mother's hand on his shoulder.

"Can you hurry back to the hut and get my mask and flippers, Ruben?" she asked. "I'm going out on the search boat."

Ruben stepped back from his mother as if jolted by an electric current. He shook his head and held up his hands. The tremendous fear running through his body left him speechless.

"What's the matter?" his mother asked at her son's panic-stricken face. "You look as though you've seen a phantom." She paused as a thought struck her. Her eyebrows narrowed in concern. "Did you have one of your bad dreams, sweetheart?"

But Ruben could not answer. He turned and ran from the pier to the hut, trying to tell himself that the dream he'd had of the men on the *Santa Maria* was only a coincidence . . . just like the dream he'd had last night. There had to be many fishing boats named after that saint, and there were countless twenty-five-foot boats manned by stern-faced captains. And, yes, even though his mother had dark hair—just like the woman swallowed by the shark in his nightmare—his dreams were nothing more than that—just dreams.

Still, no matter how hard he tried to explain them away, Ruben couldn't help but fear his dreams had become windows to the future. Taking his time in the hut, he hoped that the boat might leave on its mission without his mother. That way his dream couldn't come true. But then his mother suddenly stepped through the curtain door of the hut with a very angry look on her face.

"The lieutenant says the area we need to search is far away. If we don't leave soon, there won't be enough light to search for more than an hour at the spot." She put her hands on her hips and looked at Ruben sternly. "Now, you listen to me, Ruben. I want you to stop this nonsense this instant. I've got to leave—*now*."

"Mama, do you have to go? Can't someone else go?" Ruben babbled, his voice shaking. "Where's Papa? He wouldn't let you go if he were here."

Dr. Ortiz walked over to her son and hugged him. "Papa has gone to the hut of a village grandfather to interview him. Some people say that the old man has seen the Miocene great white and lived to tell about it. And, no—your father would not try to stop me from going to help search for the missing boat. In fact, he would come along as well."

Ruben held his mother tightly. "Please, Mama, I am afraid. I—I had a dream that—"

But his mother only smiled and pressed her index finger across Ruben's lips. "Sssh. You dream too much, my son. I'll be back before your head hits the pillow tonight—so stop worrying so much." And with that the dark-haired woman ruffled her son's hair, picked up her flippers and mask, and left Ruben standing in the hut.

Walking to the tiny window, Ruben watched as his mother walked out to the pier. There, she loaded her air tank onto the boat. The sun had moved overhead and was casting an orange glow on the water as the boat sped away, skipping over the waves like a stone.

The sun is rising as Ruben dives to twenty feet, following his father. The aquamarine water is warmer than a spa. Ruben wears only his swimsuit. His father wears his bright red rubber wet suit top over his trunks.

At first, Ruben cannot understand why the ocean water is so warm. Then he realizes that the volcanic shelf thirty feet below acts like a heating coil. It is the warmth of the Earth's ancient inner core that allows plankton to grow and attracts the many fish he sees skittering past his mask.

Suddenly Ruben sees the dark ocean floor begin to move. An earthquake, he thinks, but why is there no loud rumbling? He clamps down on his mouthpiece in panic as the ocean floor rises to meet him.

But it is not the ocean floor that is moving—it is a shark, a shark so large that its greenish back resembles an underwater mountain. Awed by the sight, Ruben's father has stopped swimming and turns back toward him. Their eyes meet, and Ruben sees his own terror reflected in his father's mask.

Megamouth opens its jaws and Ruben feels his body being sucked down into the cavernous opening of its mouth. Teeth bigger than shovel blades, bristling in razor-sharp rows like soldiers at attention, wait to liquefy him.

The creature's unblinking eye, bigger than a soccer ball, stares coldly as Ruben is drawn screaming to his death. He feels the crushing bite, watches the jagged teeth cutting through his flesh . . . then all is blackness.

"Ruben! Ruben! Wake up, son!" Reynaldo Ortiz's voice was on the edge of hysteria as he bent over his son. "Your mother has not returned! We must go out to search for her!"

Ruben's eyes were open and his mouth was locked in a half-yawn . . . or was it a soundless scream?

"Ruben!" the boy's father cried, his hand shaking as it held a smoky kerosene lantern over the bed. "Ruben, what's wrong with you? Wake up, son!" He bent close to the boy, then frantically began searching for a pulse. There wasn't even a single beat. But how could this be? There were no marks on his son's body. Still, it was cold . . . very cold.

Screaming like a madman, Reynaldo Ortiz ran to the pier and threw his scuba equipment into an old wooden boat tied there. He jumped aboard and started the engine, tears streaming from his eyes. At the last moment, just before he untied the line, he reached back onto the pier and grabbed the top of his wet suit. He zipped the bright red rubber wet suit top up to his neck to guard against the morning chill and sped into the western darkness, crying first his wife's name . . . and then his son's.

OLD WHITETIP

I am an old man now, with white hair and deep lines in my face. I have lived all my life—more than sixty-five years—on Bora Vatu, a green speck in the endless sea that tourists who come here call the South Pacific.

I am not rich, but my life is good. I grow pineapples and sugarcane on my small farm outside of Turka, the only town on our island. At dawn each day I rise and awaken my grandson, Manu, who has lived with me since my son and daughter-in-law passed on. He is a good boy, strong for one who is only fifteen.

Manu and I load our small cart with coconuts, pineapple, and sugarcane. We push the wooden cart down the bumpy main road to the large dock in front of the Royal Turka Hotel, the largest building on Bora Vatu. There we split coconuts and drink their honeyed milk and eat their tough white meat. We cut pineapples into small squares and let each piece burst in our mouths. And finally we peel the cane stalks back to their soft hearts and let their sweet juices dribble down our chins.

We sell these luscious snacks to tourists who hurry to the dock in the mornings. Many wear flowered shirts and most are covered with white smelly paste they use to block the sun. Some take catamaran tours around our island, while others rent small boats for sightseeing or fishing in the giant lagoon that stretches from the dock to the reef's edge, nearly half a kilometer away.

Over many years I have become used to the loud voices and the rude manners of a great number of tourists. They do not know and do not care about our ways on Bora Vatu. It does not bother me any longer when they shout "Hey, man," or put their hands all over my goods and push money under my nose. But Manu hates being treated like this. Some days, as we push our cart home, he tells me of his plans to leave Bora Vatu, to go to Samoa or to America.

"There is nothing here, Grandfather Mosi," he says. "What will I do? Be a waiter or a guide? I don't want to live my life taking orders from tourists. What kind of life is that?"

"There is always the farm, Manu," I tell him. "Your father and grandmother are gone. The land will be yours when my time comes."

Manu tries to hide his feelings when I say this, but I know that he does not want to remain here. He does not want to live off the land. He does not want to fish for snapper and bonito. He has never learned to swim with the sharks as we did when I was a child. Manu does not believe in the old ways.

Manu's mother and father—my son, Langa, and his wife, Tupu—were the same way. They saw the bright two-engine seaplanes filled with people whose money poured from their pockets. They studied the shiny pictures in magazines at every hotel gift shop. They watched movies and TV shows from America. And soon Langa and Tupu began to talk about leaving Bora Vatu. They talked of moving to Hawaii, to follow their dreams.

Finally, when my dear wife—Manu's grandmother—died, and I no longer had the strength to argue that the old ways were better, I gave my blessing to Langa and Tupu. And within the month they left for Hawaii. Tupu carried Manu, who was just a baby, in her arms as she boarded the tiny seaplane behind my son. They would fly, along with perhaps a dozen tourists, to Samoa. And from there they would take a small jet to their new life in Honolulu.

I can never forget that awful day. I was gathering sea slugs in the lagoon as I watched the plane lift off the ground. And then suddenly I heard the engine cough. My heart jumped to my throat as the plane tumbled from the sky, falling toward the waters past the lagoon where the reef meets the ocean and drops off into darkness.

Screaming, I ran to the water's edge. In the distance I could see the plane in pieces and bodies floating in the surf. Rescuers on the dock leaped into boats to look for survivors. And I took my canoe, paddling with all my strength, while I prayed with all my might for the gods to save my son, Tupu, and Manu.

But sharks arrived before me, drawn by the blood that poured from all the broken bodies. Horrified, I watched the beasts tear at the flesh, and then I saw two screaming tourists who had been thrown clear of the wreckage. They splashed as they floated like jellyfish in their life jackets, and I knew what they did not know—that their fear would draw the sharks. And it did.

Sickened, all I could do was watch as the hungry creatures rose up under them . . . and pulled them beneath the pinkish foam.

Then, amid the death and scattered wreckage, I saw him—Old Whitetip. His body was much larger than I had remembered, longer and wider than my canoe. Slowly he circled the clear water beneath me, then rose, his white-tipped dorsal fin breaking the surface just in front of my bow. I prayed that his glowing triangle would lead the way to my family.

My prayers were answered . . . but only in a small way. Miraculously Old Whitetip guided me through the broken bodies, paying no attention to the frenzy of his fellow scavengers. As I followed the huge white-edged fin, I searched frantically for any sign of Langa, Tupu, or Manu.

At last I heard the high-pitched cry of a baby. There, just above Old Whitetip's snout, floated the dead but untouched bodies of my son and his wife. And in the water, wailing as he dog-paddled next to his mother, was Manu—already a strong swimmer, like all people of Bora Vatu.

I gave thanks as I scooped up my grandson, held him in my arms for a long moment, then laid him in my canoe. Then I cried as I pulled the bodies of Langa and Tupu into my craft. I turned toward shore as the rescuers arrived, firing their rifles to kill the sharks who continued to feed mercilessly. And as for Old Whitetip, he silently slipped beneath the cold waves and vanished into the darkness beyond the reef, as if somehow he sensed the hatred.

I have told Manu the story of his rescue many times in the years that he has lived with me. As a child he begged me to tell it again and again. But now my young grandson is nearly a young man, and he scoffs at me when I speak of Old Whitetip.

"I am too old to believe in fairy tales, Grandfather," he tells me. "Old Whitetip is nothing but a silly myth."

Though I don't mention Old Whitetip to my disbelieving grandson anymore, the grand shark is forever in my mind. As I work, as I eat, as I sleep, Whitetip is there.

Yesterday, as Manu and I closed up our cart and prepared to walk back to the farm, I thought again of Old Whitetip and smiled. But my smile faded when I looked over at my grandson and saw storm clouds crossing his dark, handsome face.

"You look so troubled, Manu," I said. "Tell me, what is wrong?"

"Wrong?" He nearly spat the word. "Much is wrong, Grandfather. I am—"

But before Manu could finish spouting out his anger, an earsplitting explosion echoed across the lagoon. I looked out over the water and saw two young men laughing and slapping each other on the back several hundred meters away.

"Those men stopped to buy pineapple before they rented a boat," Manu said, his voice taut with anger. "Did you see what one of them was carrying in his camera case?"

"No," I replied, still shaken by the blast. "I was busy serving snacks and making change."

"It was filled with firecrackers, Grandpa Mosi," Manu said. "*Large* firecrackers. They called them M-80s. I heard them talking when they were getting ready to go fishing."

Suddenly another loud explosion ripped across the water, then another and another. I squinted my old eyes at the young men and saw them jerking fish over the side of their rented boat and laughing as they gutted them with large knives.

"Dock your boat immediately!" the constable on duty shouted through his bullhorn. "I order you to stop at once and return your boat to the dock!"

Manu shook his head in disgust. "The constable sounds angry, but he is toothless."

I nodded sadly at my grandson as I closed up the cart. It hurt me to see one so young be so downcast. Yet I knew Manu was right. He muttered under his breath as we walked along the water's edge toward home. I wanted to console him, but I had no answers.

"The hotel owners will talk to the magistrate and explain how important tourists are to Bora Vatu's economy," Manu complained. "The men will be warned but not punished. People listen when money speaks, Grandpa Mosi," he said angrily to me. "They turn deaf ears to reason."

As I took in Manu's words, I gazed out at the turquoise water. The young men who had been setting off the firecrackers were now piloting their small motor boat toward the dock. The stink of firecracker smoke and dead fish drifted onshore as they tied their craft down under the watchful eyes of the constable. Every now and then the uniformed officer blew his whistle and waved away curious onlookers.

Then I saw that one of the slaughtered fish was a young white-tipped reef shark. It was one of the many that shared the waters with us, the kind that I swam with as a child. Tears filled my weary eyes.

"What do you see, Grandpa Mosi?" Manu asked, his voice softening as he saw my sadness.

I looked into my grandson's face. "The explosions and the dead shark have recalled a lost memory, Manu."

"Tell it to me, Grandfather," Manu said, his eyes searching mine.

"It is what you call one of my 'fairy tales,'" I replied, unable to hide the bitterness in my voice. "It is nothing but a silly myth."

"I want to hear it," Manu said tenderly. "Please, Grandpa Mosi, tell me your memory."

And so, as we made our way home, I told Manu of a time long past on Bora Vatu, a time before hotels and tourists . . . and firecrackers.

"It happened more than fifty years ago," I began. "It was during the time of the great war, and I was a boy, younger than you are now, but I remember it clearly. Because the lagoon was too shallow for warships, and the island too hilly for airplanes to land, the war almost passed us by. But Japanese soldiers did land on Bora Vatu as they made their way across the Pacific. After filling their supply boats with our crops, they burned the fields and destroyed most of the huts in our village."

"Why did they do that?" Manu asked, his eyes wide as a child's.

I had no answer, so I merely continued.

"My mother and father fled to hillside caves, and my brothers and sisters and I went with them," I said, my eyes dark with memory. "As the war dragged on, I could sometimes make out the shapes of ships on the far horizon. I also heard the loud, thunderous noise of the American fighter planes as they passed overhead, chasing Japanese forces back to their homeland.

"Then, early one morning, as I was spearfishing from my canoe in the lagoon, I heard a rumble that shook the water and filled my head with a terrible sound. Trembling, I looked up to see a large airplane trailing black smoke and flames. It flew so low over the treetops that I could see American stars painted under the wings and a jagged hole in its side. The shadow of the plane passed over me like a giant bird and I could see that it had no guns."

"It must have been a cargo plane, though, wasn't it, Grandfather?" Manu asked.

I nodded. "Yes," I replied, pleased that my grandson was listening. "The plane skidded and bounced along the surface of the water. Finally it stopped at the edge of the reef in a cloud of steam and smoke. Some crew-men climbed onto the wing and jumped into the water, others stayed in the plane and tossed crates out through the big hole into a large rubber raft.

"Mesmerized, I watched from the cliffs. Suddenly the waves swallowed the plane like it was no more than a minnow. All that remained was a raft filled with crates, and five frightened men, crying pitifully for help.

"Even from the distant cliffs I could feel their fear as the men tried to push the raft toward land. I wanted to get my canoe and paddle out to them, but I knew that the sharks would soon feel their fear as I had. Still, despite my family's protests, I ran toward the men. I had to try to do something."

"And did you save them, Grandpa Mosi?" Manu asked, although he already knew the answer.

I shook my head. "The sharks struck as I neared the splashing men. There was a horrible scream and one man was gone in a bloody fountain of foam. Seeing my approach, the others swam toward me, their eyes wild with fear. But my canoe was small and could not hold so many men, so I made a wall by steering it between the survivors and their comrade, for he was already torn apart and beyond help."

"Weren't you afraid, Grandfather?" Manu asked.

"I felt no fear," I replied, not with pride but because it was simply the truth. "I knew sharks well, and they knew me. Sensing that it was *my* paddle in the water, the creatures turned from their feeding and gathered around, bumping the wood in greeting. To give the airmen time to reach shore, I paddled my canoe toward the outer edge of the reef, herding the sharks with me. Then, as I turned back to Bora Vatu, I tossed my catch to my friends as a gift."

"So you did save the men, Grandpa Mosi," Manu said.

I nodded, but the memory only filled me with tremendous sadness. "The surviving men were grateful to me, Manu, but they were also bitter about the loss of their comrade. As I helped them unload heavy crates from the raft, they spoke angrily of sharks, calling them 'bloodthirsty beasts' and 'murdering savages.' But I was young and shy toward outsiders, and I did not defend my friends, as I should have."

"It is not your fault, Grandfather," Manu said gently. "You were only a boy."

"Nevertheless, Manu," I replied, "I should have acted." I paused for a moment to gather my thoughts, then continued. "By the end of that day, the airmen had built palm-leaf shelters and set up camp at the edge of the lagoon, near where the dock stands today. And, because it is our way on Bora Vatu, the people of my village supplied the men with fresh food and water. I, too, felt it was my duty to help them, though what they had said about the sharks had angered me. And so I stood by their shelters like a servant boy, ready to run errands or serve them in any way that I was able."

"I would have let them fend for themselves," Manu said defiantly.

"It is our custom to help strangers, Manu," I replied, then went on with my tale. "As night fell, and the four men cooked fish they had been given by our villagers, I remained quietly at the edge of their fire, listening to them talk. I learned that the plane had flown far from main supply lines, and that it might be many weeks before the men could be rescued.

"At sunrise the next morning, I gathered fresh fruit and brought it to the camp. When I arrived, I saw that two airmen had built a square platform from palm logs and placed it on top of the rubber raft. They had already paddled the large float to the middle of the lagoon, and I guessed that they planned to fish from it. But I saw no spears, lines, or nets. Then I saw one man lift a green object about the size of a small pineapple and hold it high for all on shore to see.

"'Hey, chief!' the man shouted. 'Watch me go fishing with grenade bait!'

"The man yanked a small piece of metal from the side of the object and tossed it far across the clear water. Seconds later a terrible blast rang through the air and sent a plume of water high into the air. I covered my ears, but I wish I had covered my eyes, as well. For what I saw next made me sick to my stomach. It looked like the sky was raining dead fish."

I shook my head, as I saw that the tears in my own eyes had traveled into Manu's. "As the two men on the raft paddled to gather their catch, the other men on shore were laughing like hyenas. I tried to hide the unhappiness on my face, but when I saw that one crate near the shore was filled with dozens of grenades, I could not hide my sorrow. A stab in my heart made me wince, for I could feel the pain my friends beneath the water would soon feel. And I prayed that these men would be rescued from Bora Vatu so we could return to our quiet ways. Then I set off in my canoe with my nets and spears.

"I paddled across the lagoon past the edge of the reef, far away from the airmen. The shark spirit smiled on me and I filled my canoe with enough fish for my family. But as I turned back toward home, the blast of grenades sounded across the water again and again. I paddled quickly to the lagoon and heard hoots of laughter.

"How could they want even more fish, I wondered, amazed at their hunger not for food but for their sick pleasures. Then, because I was afraid of the explosions, I remained on the far side of the lagoon and watched the men on the raft. I could not believe what I saw."

"What was it, Grandfather?" Manu asked, a look of disgust on his face.

"The two men from the morning had been joined by their companions," I answered. "At first I could not make out exactly what they were doing, but suddenly I became aware of sharks passing beneath me, rushing into the lagoon.

"I looked at the raft and saw one man tie a large, bloody fish to a line. Another took a grenade from a small canvas bag and slid it inside the fish, looping the line around the metal pin that made the murderous pineapple explode when it was pulled. Then the man tossed the bait far away from the raft."

"And the sharks were drawn by the blood," Manu said, shaking his head.

"Yes," I replied. "Seconds after the shark swam away with its prize, the grenade exploded. A huge fountain of water gushed toward the heavens and water rippled across the lagoon, carrying with it the shredded body of a sleek whitetip.

"And it only got worse. After this first kill, the real slaughter began. More whitetips, drawn by the blood, swam into the lagoon. Maddened by the blood, they began to snap wildly at anything near them, sometimes killing their own.

"Laughing, the men took turns tossing out more deadly bait. The noise and the slaughter drove the people of the village back to their huts in fear, and all I could do was watch helplessly from the far side of the lagoon, afraid to paddle my canoe into the bloody waters."

I stopped for a moment and looked at my grandson. He was weeping as I had wept on that day. "This is how the men sought revenge for their fallen comrade," I told him. "But that is not the end of my story."

"What happened, Grandpa Mosi?" Manu asked, his tears flowing freely.

"Suddenly I sensed an enormous shadow passing beneath me, heading toward the men in the raft," I went on. "I looked down into the clear water and saw the outline of a shark so large that my canoe could have

easily rested on its back. The edges of the creature's fins glowed a brighter white than the inside of an oyster shell. It was as if in this one creature was the spirit of every shark that had fallen that day."

I paused for a moment. "What happened next is carved deeply in my mind," I began again nearly at a whisper, for when I spoke of Old Whitetip, I spoke only in a reverent tone. "It was an amazing sight, Manu. The huge shark rose to the surface, its dorsal fin breaking the water, and its body crossed the lagoon with a few strokes of its tail. The men on the rafts did not see the creature, so absorbed were they in their killing.

"Then one man cried out in surprise as he pointed at the water, unable to speak. The others looked where he pointed, and their eyes widened as they saw the great dark shape of the shark rushing toward them, its dorsal fin slicing the water like a saw blade. In the instant before colliding, the giant whitetip's fin disappeared under the raft.

"What made the shark stop its attack, Grandfather?" Manu asked.

I smiled at my grandson. "Old Whitetip didn't stop his attack," I replied with a sly grin. "No, he took a piece of the grenade bait and spat it out directly under the raft!"

"Yeah, right," Manu said skeptically.

I shrugged. "All I know, Grandson, is that suddenly a huge explosion echoed across the lagoon scattering body parts and splinters of palm logs everywhere. The force of the blast knocked the pins loose from a few remaining grenades, and they also began to explode. Then, as though a storm had passed, the lagoon was quiet again, quiet except for the splashing of sharks as they rose to feast on the shattered bodies of the airmen."

Manu rolled his eyes. "Old Whitetip saves the day!" Manu cried, laughing. "That's a good story, Grandpa Mosi. I have to admit you had me going there, but a kamikaze shark? I don't think so."

"I understand your disbelief, Manu," I said. "I, too, wondered about the giant shark that had blown itself to pieces. How could the beast have known about the evil game the men were playing? It was then that I truly understood the great power of the shark spirit.

"For no sooner had questions about this gigantic shark passed through my mind than I saw its huge, glowing dorsal fin, covered with palm splinters and dark red blood, break the surface. The great shark was *not* dead. It moved slowly through the carnage, leaving the feeding to its smaller brothers and sisters.

"In awe, I watched the giant pass directly beneath my canoe, close enough for me to run my hand along its rough skin. It swam out past the reef, its outline growing smaller in the distant water, until finally all I could see were the white tips of its fins glowing like stars fallen to the sea."

By the time I finished my story, Manu and I had reached the farm. "That shark, who I call Old Whitetip," I said quietly, "is the same shark that led me to you."

Manu looked into my eyes and I could sense that he wanted to believe in the spirit. But I also knew that my grandson had not grown up with the old ways and so did not believe in the powers of the shark.

Seeing this, I hurried to my room while Manu washed down the cart. I pulled out a dusty wooden box from beneath my mattress and took it outside to show my grandson.

"What do you see inside this box, Manu?" I asked him, taking off the lid.

"Four flat pieces of metal on chains, Grandpa Mosi," Manu said. "And there are names and numbers stamped on them."

"They are called dog tags, Manu," I explained. "Americans wore them during the war. I found them in my net months later while I was fishing in the lagoon."

Showing the dog tags to my grandson planted the seed of belief in him. And now this morning, sitting on the dock as the sun rises, I am certain that soon Manu will never doubt the spirit of the shark again.

For the two foolish tourists who threw firecrackers into the lagoon yesterday stopped again to buy fruit and sugarcane a short time ago. They hurried to rent a boat much like the one they had rented before, and I saw them set off across the lagoon.

I do not know whether they plan more cruelty today. But as I look toward the far side of the lagoon, ahead of their path, these old eyes see points of light beneath the water. The points are moving toward the lagoon, toward the rented boat, moving like bright stars shooting beneath the endless space of sea.

NO MORE BULL

Summer vacation was already almost over. As Steve Dill watched his fishing bobber rise and fall in the gentle swells of Muswell Pond, he had a sick feeling in the pit of his stomach—a sick feeling called *going back to school*. Yes, in just a few weeks he'd be back at Medfield Middle School starting the eighth grade, cooped up indoors when he'd much rather be fishing or watching the Yankees play. Even worse, Steve knew that Forrest Post was going to be there, just waiting to make his life miserable.

Maybe it was the kid's goofy name that warped his personality. The way Steve figured it, if he had a first name that made people want to yell "Timber!" and a last name that made people think "dumb as a . . ." Steve *himself* might turn out to be a mental case, too.

At any rate, what it *did* make Forrest Post turn into was a bully. Everyone in eighth grade agreed on that. After all, Forrest was bigger and stronger and meaner than any kid in school, and he'd been in about a million fights. That's what he claimed, anyway, and no one had the guts to question him about it.

Steve, for one, thought that all Forrest did was get into fights, look for someone to punch out, or get in trouble for having just beaten up someone. After all, the only time Steve ever saw him, Forrest was either stalking some victim, breaking somebody's nose, or sitting outside of Principal Sidoti's office waiting for his latest punishment.

Consequently just about everyone had had some kind of a painful run-in with Forrest Post, and there wasn't anyone in the eighth grade who didn't hate the guy. As far as Steve's experience went, his encounter with Forrest wasn't as painful as it was embarrassing.

"The Postman," as everyone called the bully, had decided to impress Danielle Loomis, the head cheerleader, by throwing Steve into the cafeteria Dumpster—headfirst! To this day, the incident brought tears of humiliation and disgust to Steve's eyes, and he thought he'd *never* get the smell of rotten fruit, sloppy joes, and gross Jell-O mold out of his nostrils. Principal Sidoti had suspended Forrest for the nasty stunt, but that only made him look bigger in the eyes of a lot of kids—and Steve smaller.

But it actually wasn't Forrest's meaness that really bothered Steve. No, the thing that *really* bugged Steve more than anything else was that Forrest was more than a bully—he was a know-it-all as well. You couldn't tell the guy *anything* he didn't already know. As far as Forrest was concerned, he was *never* wrong. You could show him an encyclopedia, an atlas, an almanac, or the *Guinness Book of World Records*, point to the exact words, illustration, or photograph that *proved* he was wrong, and all he'd do was wave his hand like he was brushing away a fly.

"So what?" he'd say in his froggy voice. "That doesn't mean a thing." Then he'd look you in the eye and growl, "You're not saying I'm *wrong*, are you?"

And so most kids stayed away from The Postman. Steve and his best friend, Billy Zukowski, usually crossed to the other side of the street when they saw the tall blond-haired bully coming their way. Either that, or they acted like they were so preoccupied with a deep conversation that they couldn't be bothered by him. And if all else failed, they pretended that they just plain didn't *see* the guy. Whatever it took to avoid any kind of confrontation with Forrest was what Steve and Billy did, and that's exactly what they planned to do this coming school year.

But on that very hot and steamy August afternoon, as Steve sat next to Billy and the two lazily watched their fishing lines sway in the breeze that gently blew across Muswell Pond, neither teenager was really thinking much about the next school year or keeping Forrest Post at bay. Or at least they weren't once they heard about the foot.

It was definitely one of the hottest days in August when word about the foot first reached Steve and Billy. The boys were fishing at their usual spot on Muswell Pond, a man-made body of water about the size and shape of a big oval football field. Its banks were steep—about a four-foot drop to the water—but the pond itself was shallow at the edges and no more than waist deep. The water dropped off quickly in the middle, though, and went as deep as thirty feet in some spots.

Excavated in a bowl-shaped field years before either Steve or Billy were born, the pond had a thick concrete wall at one end to contain the water that flowed in from several creeks. Without this wall, downtown Medfield would be flooded when a heavy snowfall melted or when the torrential rains came that often hit the area.

At the other end of the pond was a smaller concrete wall with a ten-foot-diameter pipe running through it well below the surface. The water that flowed through this underwater pipe fed into Muswell Brook, a channel of water which flowed lazily southeast, twisting and turning twenty miles to Wading River. From there the river widened and emptied into the Atlantic Ocean at Green Bank, several miles north of Atlantic City on the New Jersey shore.

"Nothing biting this afternoon," Steve said, reeling in his line and casting it in a different direction toward a clump of rushes about fifteen feet to his right. "It's too hot, and the bass are probably in the middle of the pond where there's deeper and cooler water."

"Yeah," Billy agreed, trying to untangle a snarl in his line. "But there could be some perch in the reeds. They feed close to the surface—and they're *always* hungry."

The boys fished in their usual relaxed way, tossing out hooks baited with fat night crawlers, then sitting under the shade of a huge scrub oak. They waited for a bite, their tanned legs dangling off the bank, and their shirtless backs protected from the blazing sun by the canopy of gnarled branches above. Content, the boys listened to the Yankees on an old transistor radio that Billy's grandfather had found at a yard sale.

Poppy Z, as everyone knew him, had raised Billy ever since Billy's folks died in a boating accident eight years ago. He was full of a million stories about the "good old days," and he'd mesmerize Billy and Steve for hours recounting them.

Steve loved coming over to the old man's Odds and Ends shop, filled with what most townspeople called junk but he called treasures. There he'd examine all the broken clocks, radios, lawnmowers, ancient-looking record players, black-and-white televisions, and rusted bicycles as he listened to Poppy Z's stories. Steve heard the tales over and over again, and he still looked forward to hearing them. He also couldn't wait to eat tons of kielbasa and galumpkes and all the other delicious Polish foods that Poppy Z cooked.

Billy and Steve were half-asleep, worn out by the hot sun and growing bored because the fish weren't biting, when the ballgame they were listening to was cut off by static from the local radio station.

We interrupt this broadcast for a bulletin from the WCNJ newsroom. The radio announcer's voice sounded tinny coming from the old 1960s radio. *We've just received word that a fisherman, who was casting at Green Bank late this morning, reeled in a severed human foot. It was found in a rubber fishing boot, approximately size ten and a half, and police believe that it may belong to Michael Sidoti, a resident of Medfield. The principal at Medfield Middle School, Sidoti was last seen by school officials one week ago, when he left for a fishing trip in the vicinity of Lyme Landing, north of Green Bank.*

Medical examiners have refused to speculate on how the foot was separated from Sidoti's body, but witnesses at the scene tell WCNJ news that the jagged edges of the boot and splintered bone of the upper ankle indicate that the victim may have been struck by a boat propeller. Stay tuned to

WCNJ for further details. We now return you to the game in progress.

The game returned with the crack of a bat and the roar of the crowd, but Steve and Billy were too shocked to listen to it. Instead, they stared straight ahead at their bobbers, each one recalling the times he had seen the principal standing in the back of a classroom monitoring a teacher's performance, giving announcements before pep rallies in the school auditorium, or pulling Forrest Post off some poor kid and yelling into the bully's smirking, pimply face.

"Gosh, poor Mr. Sidoti!" Steve finally gasped. "I mean, he was an okay guy. I mean, sure, he called my mom once and told her I wasn't working hard enough, but man . . ."

"Yeah, *nobody* deserves to go *that* way!" Billy exclaimed, shaking his head. "Not even—"

"Not even *who?*" a low, froggy voice called out from the chest-high weeds behind them.

Startled, Steve and Billy whirled around to see the hulking body of Forrest "The Postman" Post emerging from the undergrowth a few feet behind them. With The Postman were the only two guys willing to hang around him—pudgy Ed Lewis and curly-haired Chester Ray. Steve and Billy called them Forrest's "postal employees" behind their backs, since they pretty much did what Forrest told them to do—such as smash mailboxes, swipe candy, and hold down Forrest's victims.

Scrambling to his feet to reel in his line, Steve looked over his shoulder and noticed someone else with the three boys—Danielle Loomis. *What's she doing with those goons?* he wondered, his heart sinking as he remembered that it was Danielle who Forrest had been trying to impress on that fateful day he took a Dumpster dive. *How could she even be near them?*

Steve had always had a big crush on Danielle, a red-haired, freckle-faced young girl who lived about two blocks from his house. But ever since that horrible day when he'd gotten a face full of sloppy joes, Steve went red with embarrassment every time he saw her. Even now he couldn't look her in the eye.

"So, what were you guys talking about?" Forrest growled, moving toward Steve and Billy. "Not even *who* deserves to go *what* way?"

Steve swallowed hard as his eyes fell on Forrest's muscular arms. It looked like Forrest's bulging biceps had grown even bigger over the summer. Thick veins jutted out like snakes from the ball-shaped muscles in his upper arms, and the black leather bands Forrest always wore to look tough seemed like they'd grown too tight for his beefy wrists.

"We were talking about Mr. Sidoti," Billy answered calmly, standing up to face the bully.

"That geek?" Forrest sneered. "I'd like to beat the crap out of him. And I would, too—if he wasn't the principal."

"Didn't you hear?" Steve asked. "Someone hooked a human foot this morning at Green Bank. The cops think it might belong to Mr. Sidoti. We just heard it on the radio."

Forrest and his buddies burst out laughing. There were high-fives all around. Only Danielle appeared to be shocked, and Steve was relieved to see she wasn't joining the other three in their cruel celebrating.

Then Forrest abruptly stopped laughing. He reached down and grabbed Billy's radio. "Hey, where'd you get this piece of junk?" he asked, turning the dial.

"It's my grandfather's," Billy answered, reaching to take it back.

But Forrest held the radio at arm's length as the tinny voice of a broadcaster came on. "Not so fast, big shot," the bully sneered. "I want to hear the news about Sidoti myself."

This just in to the WCNJ newsroom. Police have now positively identified the human foot pulled ashore this morning at Green Bank as that of 39-year-old Michael Sidoti of Medfield. Sidoti, the principal at Medfield Middle School, has been missing for more than a week.

A spokesperson for the family says that Sidoti left last Thursday to go fishing on Wading River at Lyme Landing. Unnamed sources at the scene have told WCNJ that the tooth of a very large fish, possibly a shark, was found in the bottom of the boot. Stay tuned to WCNJ for further details.

"YYYesssss!" Forrest shouted, pumping his fist as though he'd hit a home run. "Good riddance to a total jerk! Hah! He probably made the shark barf!"

Chester and Ed thought this was hysterically funny, but Danielle merely looked at the ground.

"Uh, when you're finished being totally obnoxious, would you mind giving back my radio?" Billy asked, taking a step toward Forrest.

Steve thought his friend had gone crazy and watched as the bully stopped laughing and stared coldly at Billy.

"You like to fish so much, go fish!" Forrest yelled. And with that, he tossed the radio into the pond. It plopped in about six feet out and sank like a stone.

In a split second, Billy was nose-to-nose with the bully. "What did you do that for, you jerk?" he shouted, his cheeks reddening. "That's my grandfather's radio! You'd better—"

But before Billy could even finish his threat, Forrest planted both of his big hands on the boy's chest and shoved him hard. Surprised by the sudden push, Billy stumbled backward, completely off balance. He tried to regain his footing, but it was no use—he slipped on the steep, slick bank and fell into the water.

"I'd better what?" Forrest sneered, standing over Billy as he spat out mouthfuls of murky water. Then, as an afterthought, the bully turned toward Steve. "Hey, why don't you go help your friend?" he asked.

"What's the matter, Stevie?" Chester taunted. "Don't you know how to swim?" He took a menacing step toward Steve.

"Oh, he's a *good* swimmer!" Ed exclaimed, moving in next to Chester. "I saw him go Dumpster diving!"

Steve felt his ears burn as Danielle burst out in a high-pitched giggle. Then before he knew what was happening, Ed and Chester were on him, picking him up and tossing him into the pond as far out as Forrest had pitched the radio.

Mortified, Steve scrambled over to Billy, and the two just watched in silent humiliation as their tormentors turned and ran off, Danielle right behind them.

"Forrest will get his someday," Billy said, gritting his teeth in anger.

"Yeah," Steve mumbled. "Whatever goes around comes around."

A few hours later, back at Billy's house, the smell of kielbasa filled the kitchen. Poppy Z stood at the stove, turning the pieces of browning sausage in the frying pan, while Steve looked on with hungry anticipation. He'd borrowed a pair of Billy's gym shorts until his wet clothes dried out.

An angry scowl still on his face, Billy stood at the kitchen sink. He'd just told his grandfather the whole miserable story and apologized for being unable to retrieve the radio.

"Forget about it," Poppy Z scoffed. "I'm working on a bunch of them at the shop. I'm just glad you boys weren't hurt." He paused for a moment. "Now tell me more about this impossible shark attack you two kids heard about."

"What do you mean—*impossible*?" Billy asked with curiosity. "They found a shark's tooth in the principal's boot, Poppy Z."

"You said Mr. Sidoti had gone to Lyme Landing," the old man said. "That's at least five miles upstream from Green Bank, which isn't even salt water. Besides, there's no way a shark could make it that—"

Suddenly Poppy Z's words froze in his throat and he looked like he'd been hit by a jolt of electricity. His hands trembled as he wiped the sweat from his brow.

"What's the matter, Poppy?" Billy asked, stepping toward the trembling man.

"Oh . . . nothing," his grandfather replied slowly. "I—I just remembered something from a long time ago, that's all." He paused and looked at the boys. "It was just a story my uncle used to tell me when I was your age."

"About sharks?" Steve asked curiously.

Poppy Z nodded. "About *one* shark in particular. A killer shark." He returned his attention to the sizzling sausage on the stove. "My uncle was a doctor, and when he was in medical school he took a summer job as a lifeguard at a beach just south of Atlantic City." Poppy Z's eyes slowly misted over. "It happened in the summer of 1916, my uncle used to tell me, several years before I was even born. Hah! The story is so old I can hardly remember all the details."

"Try," Steve begged.

"Yeah, Poppy," Billy pleaded. "We want to hear it."

The old man smiled. "Well, it seems that my uncle actually witnessed a shark attack."

"Wow!" the boys gasped in unison.

"It was a hot August day. A day like this," Poppy Z went on. "A lot of people were in the water, when all of a sudden my uncle heard a horrible scream. He plunged into the surf and rescued a young man with a big chunk bitten out of his leg." Poppy Z shook his head. "I remember Uncle Stan saying that the guy was only standing in water about waist deep."

"So what happened?" Billy asked, his eyes wide. "Did your uncle do CPR on the guy?"

"Well, Uncle Stan dragged the man onto the sand while other lifeguards cleared people from the water. It was only then that my uncle got a real good look at the extent of the injury, and he could see the guy didn't have a chance. You see, the shark had taken off almost the whole front of the victim's thigh. Blood from the femoral artery was spurting like a fountain." Poppy Z again wiped sweat from his brow. "My uncle tried to plug the wound with his hands to stop the bleeding, but it was too late. The blood drained from the poor guy like water from a bathtub. He died in minutes."

Steve and Billy looked at each other. They didn't need to say anything. Each knew that the other was thinking about Mr. Sidoti.

"What brought the whole gruesome story back to me was thinking about how this shark supposedly attacked your principal in fresh water," Poppy Z went on as he dished the hot kielbasa onto three plates. "You see, Uncle Stan told me that friends of the man he saw bleed to death described the shark as a bull shark, and not long after the incident, what was believed to be that *same* creature was spotted at the mouth of the Fenton River, a few miles away. Two weeks later, the beast had made its way *thirty* miles upstream—as far as Simmsville!"

"Were there any more attacks?" Billy asked.

Poppy Z scratched his bald head. "If I remember right, the shark flipped over a rowboat and killed two kids who were fishing. It happened right where the Fenton flows through downtown. Other people were attacked, too, but they weren't killed. It caused a real panic and there was a $5,000 reward out to anyone who brought in the beast dead or alive." Poppy cut a thick slice of kielbasa and plopped it in his mouth. "Cops finally shot the monster. You can probably find stories about it in the library." He shook his head and sighed. "Boy, that was a long time ago. I must be getting old."

With only a week left before school started, Steve and Billy decided to go fishing again, despite the threat of running into Forrest Post. Unlike the last time they'd fished at Muswell Pond, however, the boys were reeling in fish by the dozens.

"I've got another one, Billy!" Steve shouted happily. "I can't believe the luck we're having today. We'll have enough bass to feed the whole town if we keep this up."

"I'll get the net," Billy offered. He had hauled in seven fish already and was taking a break, reading a book in the shade. "I can't figure out why there's so many bass this close to the surface—not to mention this close to the shore."

As Billy came over with the net, Steve continued to wrestle with the fish, and moments later, the green-and-black striped back of a smallmouth bass broke the surface. Well over two pounds, this gorgeous baby was a definite keeper.

Billy slid down the bank to the edge of the water and scooped the struggling fish out of the water. As he did, he couldn't believe what he was seeing about ten feet off shore. "Man!" he cried. "Look at 'em all!" He ripped the hook from the soft pink flesh of the bass's mouth. "You can see *dozens* of fish from this angle!"

While Steve cranked in his line, Billy scrambled up the bank with the fish. In a few minutes he had gutted and scaled the bass and put it in an ice chest that they usually brought home empty.

"I think that has to be the last fish," Billy said as he settled his back up against the tree and opened his book. "There's no more room in the chest."

Steve set his pole down and laid belly-first on the matted grass that hung over the bank. Squinting in the sunlight that reflected off the pond, he tried to look beneath the surface of the sun-dappled water. After a few minutes, his eyes adjusted and he, too, could see the huge masses of fish just a few feet below.

"Hey, I found it!" Billy suddenly called.

"Found what?" Steve called back over his shoulder.

"I got this book on shark attacks from the library, and there's a section in here called *The Deadly Summer of 1916."* He paused to scan the page. "My grandfather was right. Listen:

"No photograph of the Simmsville man-eater exists, but scientists believe that the killer is probably a bull shark. These creatures, named for the large hump of flesh directly behind the head, can grow to lengths of eight feet and weigh up to six hundred pounds. Bull sharks have been known to migrate hundreds of miles up freshwater rivers, driving schools of fish ahead of them. There are records of attacks by bull sharks occurring in water as shallow as three feet!" Billy stopped and set down the book.

"Are you thinking what I'm thinking, Billy?" Steve asked, suddenly moving away from the bank and facing his friend.

Billy nodded, his eyes wide with fear. "It's been over two weeks since Mr. Sidoti disappeared. And Poppy said that the shark in 1916 took about two weeks to make it about thirty miles or so upstream, right?"

"Right," Steve replied. "And doesn't Muswell Brook empty into Wading River?"

"Yeah, at Lyme Landing," Billy answered.

"Well, doesn't this pond feed into Muswell Brook?" Steve's voice trembled. "And aren't there an awful lot of fish out here today? I mean, more than we've ever seen before?"

Billy nodded. "Maybe we should pack up and—"

"Well, if it isn't Tom Sawyer and Huck Finn," broke in Forrest Post.

Steve felt his heart leap as he saw not only Ed and Chester following in Forrest's path through the golden-rod and bulrushes, but also Danielle bringing up the rear. Billy slammed his book shut and stood up, ready for a fight.

Forrest looked at Billy's book. "Hey, I didn't know a dweeb like you could even read. Sharks, huh? They've suddenly become my favorite animal. Hah! I'd sure like to meet the shark that ate Sidoti. In fact, I'd like to shake his fin!"

Ed and Chester joined their leader in guffaws of laughter. Danielle just looked uncomfortable.

"You might get that chance," Billy said as he began to collect his gear. "Steve and I were just talking about the possibility that there could be a shark somewhere around here. Maybe even right *here* in this pond."

Forrest shook his head in disgust. "Man, are you ever *stupid,*" he said, his froggy voice oozing contempt. "Don't you even know the difference between salt water and fresh water? Sharks don't hang out in fresh water."

"Some do," Steve blurted out. "Besides, something's driving all these fish toward the shore."

"Sorry, jerks," Forrest said. "I know sharks and there's no way Muswell Pond has anything but itty-bitty fishies in it."

Billy picked up the book and opened it. He thumbed through the pages until he found the place about the bull shark. "You want to make a bet, pal?" Billy asked, pointing to the story he'd just read to Steve.

Forrest glanced at the page, then glared at Billy. "You saying I'm wrong, Zukowski?"

Billy looked the bully squarely in the eye. "No. I'm saying the *book* says you're wrong!"

With that, Forrest kicked the book right out of Billy's hands. "You've heard of flying fish?" he asked his friends. "Well, this is a flying book!"

Ed and Chester laughed halfheartedly, and Danielle rolled her eyes as Billy went scrambling for the book . . .

right to the edge of the bank, where he lost his balance and fell into the murky pond.

"Billy!" Steve cried as Forrest and the others hooted with laughter. He reached over the edge of the bank and extended his hand to his friend, but as he did, Billy saw Chester sneaking up behind Steve, ready to push him in.

"Watch out, Steve!" Billy shouted.

Steve turned around just as Chester came rushing at him. In a flash, Steve grabbed the boy's wrist and hurled him out over Billy into the water.

"You're dead meat, Dumpster diver!" Chester yelled as he bobbed to the surface of the water.

"Revenge!" Ed yelled, running at Steve.

Running on pure adrenaline, Steve faked one way, then the other, and Ed went tumbling into the pond as well.

"Well, well, well," Forrest said, tapping his foot as he watched the whole thing. "Look at Stevie, Danielle. He's giving my boys a real run for their money." He moved toward Steve like a cat ready to pounce. "But let's see how he deals with a *real*—"

But before Forrest could finish his threat, a shrill scream split the muggy afternoon air. Forrest froze as he watched Chester's face turn into a mask of horror.

"*Aaaah! Aaaah!*" Chester screamed. He was flailing about in chest-deep water. "Something's got me!"

Still in the water, Billy and Ed were dumbfounded as they saw Chester rising up out of the pond in the monstrous jaws of a shark. Seconds later, the beast yanked the boy beneath the surface like a rag doll.

"Steve!" Billy shrieked as he frantically clawed his way up the bank. "Help!"

Steve pulled Billy partway up the slippery bank, and then he saw Ed frantically splashing toward shore. Right behind the panicked boy, a shark fin had risen to the surface and was heading right at him like a saw blade.

Quickly yanking Billy up onto the bank, Steve plunged toward Ed, who had gone rigid with fear. He stretched out his hand and grabbed the trembling boy, then using an inner strength he didn't know he had, Steve tugged Ed toward the bank.

"Billy! Forrest! Danielle!" Steve called, panting. "Help us!"

But while Billy and Danielle formed a human chain to help Steve and Ed out of the water, the biggest bully Medfield Middle School had ever seen was unable to move. His face a ghostly white, Forrest Post just stood there wagging his head from side to side and yelling, "No way! No way! No *way*!"

Fighting for his life, Steve fought his way through the sucking muck at the bottom of the pond as he held on to the hysterical boy who had tormented him only moments earlier. And then suddenly Ed started to shriek and kick wildly at the water. "Aaaah! My leg! My leg!" he screamed as the shark pulled him away from Steve.

But Steve held on, stretched between Ed, who pulled him toward the pond, and Billy and Danielle, who pulled him toward the bank. Then finally Ed managed to land a blow on the shark's sensitive snout, and the beast released its grip.

As Danielle and Billy helped Steve and the profusely bleeding Ed out of the pond, the brutal creature swam off, retreating for deeper waters.

"Get help!" Steve shouted to Forrest, who still hadn't made a move. "Now! You idiot!"

But seeing that Forrest still remained motionless, Danielle screamed that she would go and was off in a flash.

As his eyes focused on the ghastly wound in Ed's leg, now spurting blood, Steve remembered how Poppy Z's uncle had tried to save the young man who'd been attacked by the bull shark in 1916. Pulling back the ripped fabric and separating the torn piece of flesh, he thrust his fist into the jagged hole in Ed's leg, trying to stop the bleeding until help arrived.

"Do you think he's gonna make it?" Forrest suddenly asked quietly.

"No thanks to you, jerk!" Billy snapped. "If it wasn't for Steve—"

All at once sirens split the air, and moments later, rescue workers plunged through the underbrush, led by Danielle. The emergency medical technicians worked quickly, stabilizing the unconscious boy by applying a tourniquet and a pressure bandage.

"Someone must have heard us screaming," Danielle explained, her voice quivering. "They were already on their way."

As the EMTs lifted Ed onto a stretcher, one of them turned toward Steve, who stood there shaking, his fist dripping blood. "Good work, son," the man said. "I'm sorry about the other boy, but you may have just saved this boy's life."

"I—I was gonna help," Forrest cried. "Really, I—"

But sensing that no one believed him, he just sank to his knees and wept.

Steve looked over to Billy, who said nothing. Then

several loud cracks rang through the air as police sharpshooters fired their weapons at a dark shape in the pond. Within moments, the water filled with blood and the body of a small bull shark floated to the surface.

Billy looked out at the dead creature, then back at Forrest, still on his knees and sobbing.

"Hey, Steve. It looks like we won't be bothered by that bull shark anymore," he said, pointing out toward the water. "Or by that bully," he added, pointing to the boy sobbing on the bank.

FUTURE SHARK

The hiss of the door on the bio-module alerted Tess that she was not alone. Something was approaching from the outer barrier. Sensors on the control panel told her that the intruder was a carbon-based humanoid, but Tess pulled out her laser ray just in case. She'd seen too many nasty rodents on this poisoned planet. You never knew when some toothy brute might chew its way past the TC-6 sentry modules.

"Halt!" Tess shouted through the steel door that separated the lab from the outer compartments. "Identify before entry!" She tried to make her thirteen-year-old voice sound deeper and more threatening than it really was.

Suddenly a young man's voice crackled over the intercom. "Hey, little sister! Put down the laser. It's only me."

"Del!" Tess exclaimed as a young man stepped into the lab enclosure and waved his webbed fingers in greeting. "What are you doing here? I thought you were looking for food sources on Trillin!"

Del, who looked just like a male version of Tess, wrapped his arms around his sister in a brotherly hug. "I was. We finished our work there. Instead of going back, I got reassigned here to pilot the Food Transport."

Tess snuggled close to the gill slit behind Del's ear hole. Then she stood back to study the brother she hadn't seen in over three years. He was more of a parent than a brother, really. He had practically raised Tess after their parents starved to death during the Great Famine that took the lives of millions on their home planet, Vodan.

In fact, Tess knew that if it hadn't been for Del she'd still be back on that miserable, water-covered planet, and she'd never have become the youngest research scientist on the Intergalactic Food Search Expedition. It was unheard of for the Vodanian Land Lords to include an adolescent—*especially* an Under Dweller—in an off-world mission. But Del, one of the few Under Dwellers with clout, had used his influence with the Land Lords to get Tess away from Vodan. His superb navigational skills made him one of the most admired fleet pilots in the universe, and since Tess had last seen him, Del had probably been to dozens of planets in search of edible life-forms. Of course, the best specimens would belong to the Land Lords, leaving the rest to Under Dwellers.

"You're looking good, Del," Tess said approvingly. "I guess life in a different galaxy agrees with you."

"*Anyplace* but home agrees with me," Del said. "And get this—Trillin is a deserted planet and it has *dry* land with a climate perfect for soil-grown crops." He took Tess by the shoulders. "We've discovered incredible vegetables there, Tess! And *anyone* can use the land—not just Land Lords!"

"Wow!" Tess exclaimed. "You mean I may be eating something other than algae paste someday?"

Del nodded. "We were able to develop seed types that will grow in artificial light. Right now the Food Transport from Trillin is carrying those seeds *and* soil back to Vodan. If the Lords grant their approval, we can grow food right here in the Main Biosphere!" He studied his sister's laboratory surroundings. "So . . . how's your research going here on . . . what's this planet called?"

"Earth," Tess said. "That's the name we've deduced from the holographic records left behind by those who once inhabited the planet. Our research indicates that the humanoid life that once existed here became extinct back in 2097."

Del's eyes widened in amazement as he converted the numbers to Vodanian terms. "You mean to tell me that this chunk of galaxy has been vacant for more than five hundred years?"

Tess nodded. "From what we can tell, there was an atmospheric change that was brought on by fires in areas called rain forests and by vehicles powered with carbon-based fuel. It was catastrophic—the atmosphere was filled with lethal amounts of carbon monoxide and one day it suddenly reached a critical mass. Humans suffocated. Other life-forms—both in the oceans and on the land—died as well when the poisons reached toxic levels. In a way the Earthlings were lucky—they went quickly. They didn't have to suffer a creeping starvation like those on Vodan."

"What about other life-forms?" Del studied several specimens on a lab table. "Have you found anything on Earth that we might be able to transport back to Vodan for food?"

Tess shook her head. "Land-based life here consists of almost indestructible species of crawling insects and vicious furry rodents that can chew their way through just about anything. The records indicate they are called 'cockroaches' and 'rats.' They can reproduce incredibly fast, but they carry disease, therefore neither is a viable food source."

Del wrinkled his nasal opening in disgust as Tess shone a light on the floor under her work station that sent dozens of cockroaches scuttling into dark corners. "See? There they are," she said. "Those things can live almost anywhere. The planet is a virtual wasteland, but somehow cockroaches and rats are able to survive."

"Well, what about ocean life?" Del asked. "Are there any species we can transport and raise on Vodan?"

Tess shrugged. She'd spent nearly a year researching the ocean life of this dead planet, and her frustration level was at its peak. "The oceans are basically dead," she replied flatly. "We can see that there is *some* life—mainly a crustacean species—and so I'm working on breeding them so we can raise them on hydro-farms."

Tess took Del's hand and led him into an enormous domed chamber with an immense tank of water. She stood on the walkway and pointed to the bottom of the tank, crawling with six-legged creatures, each with sharp claws and green shells that were almost the same color of Tess and Del's scaly skin.

"Of course, I doubt whether these creatures are the answer to our food crisis," Tess said sadly. "They're so small and the shells are awfully hard. I mean, sure, if you're hungry, you'll eat anything . . . but what we need are large, hearty sea creatures that can be raised and harvested."

Del ran his webbed fingers through his kelp-colored hair. Tess knew that her brother was thinking of the Great Famine. It had happened after the Universe War, when Land Lords confined the Under Dwellers to domed spheres beneath the ocean.

At first, they had adapted well to life underwater. Fish were plentiful, and Under Dwellers developed gills and webbed extremities to travel more easily outside the Biospheres. But as populations above and beneath the ocean grew, food supplies shrank. The Land Lords kept the most nourishing food for themselves, leaving Under Dwellers to survive on nothing more than algae paste and a tasteless, odorless mush made out of sea slugs. Millions of Under Dwellers, mostly older citizens like Tess and Del's parents, starved to death.

"Well, if we don't find food sources at this end of the universe, we're going to die off, too," Del said, his voice cracking as he thought of his parents' slow, suffering death. "If only we could find sea creatures strong enough to survive the journey back to Vodan. Of course, if we did, the Land Lords would just confiscate them and leave the rest of us nothing."

"Not if *I* can help it," Tess said with determination. Then she grabbed Del's hand and pulled him toward the far end of the chamber. There she punched in some code numbers on a wall panel, and a hidden door suddenly slid open. "Quick, Del! Go inside!" she whispered, pushing her brother through the entrance and sealing it behind her.

"Sharr, Fina, and the others know nothing about this," she said once the door had closed. "I pretend that all my work is on breeding larger species of the shelled creatures. But most of the time I'm in here alone."

Tess pressed a button on a wall panel and one side of the room appeared to slide away, revealing a tank about twenty feet square and eight feet deep. Del looked with amazement at a four-foot-long creature frantically swimming in circles, its triangular fin slicing the water like a knife.

"Is that a . . . *fish?*" he asked, surprise in his voice. Fish were just a memory for Under Dwellers. Only the Land Lords ate fish now, and they raised the succulent, protein-rich creatures in an inland sea on the Great Island. Smacking his lips, Del remembered the taste of fish and a tear welled up in his eye. Naturally the Land Lords refused to share their food staple with those they considered to be inferior—even when those who lived beneath the sea were dying. In fact, any Under Dweller caught trying to sneak through underwater passages into the well-protected Lords' Sea were killed on the spot and fed to the fish themselves!

"It's a clone of a fish," Tess answered. "We were exploring a sector that was once called Australia, and I came to a vast underwater area designated on ancient maps as the Great Barrier Reef. While my colleagues were off looking for other land-based life, I decided to do some out-of-transport underwater exploration. As I chipped away at the mineral formations, I knocked loose a hard triangular object."

"A *tooth?*" Del asked, gazing in awe at the small but powerful creature swimming in the tank. He was only guessing, since he'd never actually seen fish with teeth. The plump orange fish raised by the Land Lords on Vodan had only soft bristle-like strainers, since all they fed on were microscopic sea life and an occasional rebel Under Dweller that had been ground up into fish meal.

"It's amazing, I know," Tess replied. "But it *is* a tooth, and I replicated its DNA to create this specimen. The results have been extraordinary. In fact, this creature nearly grew overnight in water of the same composition as that on Vodan."

"It's one of the healthiest life-forms I've seen just about anywhere in the universe," Del said, his eyes fixed on the circling creature. "What's it called?" He reached toward the water to stroke the creature's sleek dark back.

"Don't do that!" Tess cried, grabbing Del's webbed extremity before it reached the water. "It's feeding time, so you have to be very careful." She reached beneath an examination table and pulled out a metal cage. Inside was a large rat, squealing as if it sensed its fate. "The creature was known in Earthling scientific terms as *Carcharodon carcharias*. But most humanoids referred to it as the great white shark."

"Great? As in large?" Del asked. "It doesn't look very large to me. The fitapia on Vodan are much larger."

"Based on the computer projections of the tooth that I used to clone this shark, the creatures, in Earthling measurements, must have been nearly twenty feet long," Tess said, climbing on a step stool and holding the cage over the tank. "I'm not exactly certain where it ranked on the food chain, but I believe it was near the top. Watch this."

Unlatching the cage door, Tess let the plump rat tumble into the tank. It quickly sank beneath the water, then immediately surfaced, frantically paddling toward the glass as though it would claw right through it.

Del watched in amazement as the shark instantly whirled around toward the thrashing rodent. Then it dove to the bottom of the tank, turned, and propelled itself straight toward the rat, jaws wide with anticipation.

In seconds the rat's body was severed in half as the shark's razor-sharp teeth bit into it. The clear water mixed with the rat's dark red blood turned pink as the shark, now in a frenzy, rose into the air and shook the helpless rodent like a dog playing with a chew toy. Moments later, only one life-form remained in the tank.

Tess looked at her brother and smiled. She had never seen him speechless before. "Amazing, isn't it?" she said as she mopped up droplets of blood and water that had spilled onto the floor. "Commander Sharr can't understand why we don't have a rat problem here at the lab. If he only knew I've been trapping them to feed this—"

Suddenly Tess stopped. The blinking light on the wall panel indicated entry in the main tank chamber. In a flash, she closed the panel, hiding her creation. Then she quickly pushed Del out of the room in front of her.

"Please don't say anything about this, Del," Tess whispered. "If the Commander finds out what I'm doing, he'll send me back to Vodan and turn me into fish food!"

"Don't worry, sis," Del muttered, acknowledging the two Lords in the main tank room with an upraised palm. "If you can find a way to feed our citizens, I'll do anything to keep your secret."

"Greetings, Commander Sharr . . . Supervisor Fina," Tess said as she and her brother made their way along the walkway over the tank. "I'd like to introduce you to my brother, UD-5411."

The two Vodanian Lords returned Del's upraised salute. "*The* UD-5411?" Commander Sharr exclaimed. "I have heard much about your excellent navigational skills, sir."

Del nodded, his acknowledgment of the compliment. "I would have reported to you at my arrival, but the sentry unit directed me here when I punched in Tess's code," Del said, anticipating their question. "I have been assigned to pilot the Food Transport."

"We are looking forward to returning to Vodan soon, UD-5411. This barren rock of a planet has nothing of interest to us," Commander Sharr said. He trained his almond-shaped black eyes on Tess. "Working late again, UD-5412?" he asked. "How much more research do you need to do on those horrible shelled creatures? Supervisor Fina and I were just talking about how eager we are to leave Earth. There appears to be no land-based life worth harvesting on this poisoned planet."

Tess met her superiors' gaze with a mysterious smile. "My work will not last much longer," she said. "I'm trying to determine whether I can breed larger specimens. Although the meat beneath the shell is rich in nutrients, they are very small and removing the small bits of flesh from each creature would be difficult for those of us with webbed fingers." Tess never referred to herself as an Under Dweller. She hated the term.

The Land Lords looked at each other and nodded. "Very well, UD-5412," Supervisor Fina said arrogantly. "We will give you the time you need. You are clearly a gifted young scientist—for an Under Dweller—and your brother is held in high regard among our leaders. I hope both of you are grateful for our patience."

Commander Sharr nodded his agreement. "Come, Supervisor Fina, a nice fat fitapia steak awaits us." Then, looking disdainfully at the green-skinned brother and sister before him, he added, "I am sending most of the team back to Vodan. I received a transmission from the Trillin ship today. We may soon have land-grown vegetable matter to complement our fitapia. There is no need to remain here. We will make one last search of Earth, then return to Vodan. Is that clear, UD-5412?" he asked, his orange skin glistening in the artificial light.

Tess glanced at Del. This meant that she didn't have much time to perfect her cloning of the shark as a food source for her kind.

"I will do my best, Commander. My fellow . . . *Under Dwellers,*" she said, practically choking on the words, "are growing very tired of algae paste and slug mush."

Tess felt her eyes growing heavy as she leaned over and studied the rapidly growing embryo. It would soon become a viable life-form, but she knew she had little time to make it happen. She hadn't left the laboratory area in days, frantically trying to complete her mission.

Meanwhile, Del helped out by keeping Commander Sharr and Supervisor Fina distracted. He took them on dazzling flights to distant sectors of Earth and told them fascinating tales of the adventures he'd had while searching the universe for edible life-forms. Even so, Commander Sharr had already ordered most of Tess's research team back to Vodan.

Tess left her lab station and entered the huge dome that held the water tank. Moving along the walkway, she held tightly to the rail. She didn't want to lose her balance and fall in. It wasn't that she couldn't swim, of course, but now something else shared the huge tank that had once housed only the shelled creatures.

As she made her way along the enormous expanse of water, she gazed in awe at the dark shape of the giant beast gliding effortlessly under the water, its triangular fin protruding more than three feet above the surface. By feeding it practically around the clock, Tess had managed to help her shark practically double in size over the last week. Then, with her brother's help, she tranquilized the beast and moved it into the larger tank, where it continued to grow. Now the gargantuan shark was nearly four times as large and heavy as it had been when Del had first seen it.

Tess pressed a button on a control unit. A large panel slid open and all at once the dome was filled with a squealing rat nearly as large as a humanoid child. Among the other projects that had kept Tess occupied day and night was her search for food supplies to keep the great white's appetite satisfied. And one night, while working late in the lab, she accidentally stumbled on the perfect way to keep the creature content.

Although Tess usually ate in the dining quarters, because of the limited time that the Land Lords had given her, she had no time to eat anywhere but at work. One cold night, while preparing a bowl of Vodanian slug paste to eat, she dozed off. After about a three-hour snooze, Tess awoke with a start to find that somehow the artificial ultraviolet light of the lab had acted on the genetic code of the slugs.

Suddenly the amount of slug paste before her had tripled. In fact, the bowl was literally oozing over with the gooey mess. To Tess, this meant only one thing. Strictly by chance, she'd stumbled on a way to use ultraviolet light to enhance the growth of a main food staple—slugs. The question was, would it work on the shark's main food source—rats?

Rather than taking the time to expose the rats to the ultraviolet light, Tess decided just to feed the affected slug paste directly to the rodents. Sure enough, the enhanced slug mush caused the rats to double in size every few hours. Yes, the more they gorged on the growth-inducing paste, the larger they became.

The shark will love these little pigs! Tess thought.

And she had been right. The shark adored its fattened-up treats. And now, as it made quick work of its latest rodent feast, Tess's cloned beast clouded the clear water in the tank with blood and fur. Both disgusted and delighted by her progress, Tess activated the filter system to clear the water of the mess, then returned to her work.

Once again Tess's long hours had made her fall asleep at her desk, but a blinking light at her workstation jolted her awake. A life-form had entered the tank chamber. Tess shook her head to clear away the sleep, then she hurried into the large room.

"Del!" she cried, breathing a sigh of relief as she saw her brother making his way down the walkway. She ran to greet him.

"What's up, sis?" he asked. "You look excited."

"I've got fantastic news!" Tess exclaimed. "I've been able to alter the chromosomes on a skin sample from the great white. If my work goes according to plan,

we'll have a male shark to take back to Vodan along with our female. All I need is a little more time."

"There *is* no more time," Del said, his voice low and ominous. "Sharr and Fina have ordered me to prepare the Transport for departure by the next planetoid rotational sequence."

Tess's eyes widened. "But I'm not finished, Del! I need to—"

"Actually, you *are* finished, UD-5412!" a voice echoed from the far side of the domed tank room.

Tess's heart froze as she saw Commander Sharr making his way up the stairs that led to the walkway. It was only a moment before he noticed the enormous creature swiftly cruising around the tank like an underwater vehicle.

"We have been delayed long enough on this hopeless planet," the commander said impatiently as he pulled his huge flabby body up the stairs. "Supervisor Fina and I have directed UD-5411 to prepare for immediate departure. If you are not prepared to leave at the next planetary rotational sequence, you will be left behind with your cockroaches, your rats, and your—" At that moment the commander reached the walkway and looked across the great expanse of the tank. "Great Vodanian ghosts! UD-5412, I demand to know what kind of life-form is *that*? And *why,* in the name of Vod, is it in this tank?"

Tess spoke calmly as she moved toward the chubby orange-skinned commander. "It is a life-form that once existed here on Earth, sir," she said. "It was known as the great white shark, and I was able to reproduce its genetic code to create this female clone. I am now attempting to hatch a male embryo as a mate."

"And why have you told no one of this remarkable work?" Commander Sharr's hungry black eyes studied the huge creature as though it were a gourmet meal. "Creatures of this size could prove to be an absolutely extraordinary food source." He paused. "For Land Lords, of course. You'll have to bring those wretched shelled creatures back to Vodan to supply the needs of your fellow Under Dwellers."

"Sir, that is exactly why—" Tess began.

But the commander cut her off by raising his beefy hand and bellowing, "The Land Lords will decide what is the best use of your work!" He walked along the edge of the tank. "We will leave behind some sentry units and housing materials to make room for the sharks in the transport." He smiled evilly at Tess. "UD-5412, I feel that you should be disciplined for your failure to report the remarkable nature of your work. Therefore you will stay behind as well. Since the shark is clearly *Lord* food, it is best that I present it to the leadership council myself."

Tess met Del's gaze. They both knew that the time had come. "Actually, sir, I think that my brother and I will be presenting the shark," she said firmly.

"How dare you contradict me!" the commander yelled. But he suddenly stopped any further reprimand when he realized that he was alone with two Under Dwellers. He reached for a control button to summon the sentry units, but Del was faster.

"Sorry, sir!" he snarled, grabbing the commander's soft, dimpled hand. "But our new food source is hungry!"

In a flash, he and Tess lifted the heavyset body of the pompous Land Lord and heaved him over the iron railing. There was a whomping splash, and instantly the dark shape of what looked like a gigantic torpedo circled around. In seconds, it swiftly propelled toward the terrified intruder.

Outside of the tank, Tess and Del watched coldly as Commander Sharr thrashed in the jaws of the huge beast. In moments, his cries for help ceased forever as he was pulled to the bottom of the tank and shredded into orange ribbons. Then, once again, Tess pressed a button, activating the filter to clear the tank of the shark's bloody leftovers.

"I guess we've crossed the line now, little sister," Del said. "I'm afraid we can't allow *any* Land Lords to return to Vodan with us."

Tess nodded, her face reflecting the seriousness of the actions they had taken. "I suppose we should get it over with as soon as possible," she said. "Shall I go ahead and summon Supervisor Fina? We could tell him there is an emergency in the tank chamber."

Del shook his head. "No, give the shark time to digest its meal," he replied. "I'll go to Fina's quarters and tell him you've discovered a new food source. Like Commander Sharr, he'll probably race over here so *he* can be the one to take the discovery to the leadership council." Del made his way to the chamber exit. "As long as the shark keeps eating them, we can do away with the Land Lords one by one."

"How long do you suppose we have before Sharr, Fina, and the other Lords will be missed back on Vodan?" Tess asked. "Surely they will send patrols to investigate."

"I'll handle it, sis," Del replied. "I can issue a phony report of an accident in some distant sector. As long as we bring back a new food source, I can't imagine that anyone will care." He smiled at Tess, trying to reassure her. "Now, no more worrying. Pack up things and let's get off this polluted planet."

"But I'm not finished with my research," Tess insisted.

Del looked at his sister impatiently. "What's left to do, Tess? Once the male shark emerges and is healthy enough for space travel, we can breed them and raise them for food back on Vodan."

Tess looked at her brother and shook her head. "The food chain doesn't work like that. I didn't clone the sharks to serve as food, Del."

"You *didn't?*" Del couldn't believe his ears. "Well, then what *did* you create them for?"

"Listen, brother. You take care of Supervisor Fina and anyone else that gets in our way," Tess replied firmly. "I'll take care of feeding everyone back on Vodan—well, *almost* everyone," she added with a glint in her eye.

Del looked curiously at his little sister, who all of a sudden seemed so confident and powerful. Then he made his way back toward the living quarters to begin the elimination procedure.

"By the way," she said as he exited. "I'll need room for other food sources in the Transport."

Several months later, Tess greeted her colleagues and friends in the central dining area of the Main Undersea Biosphere. The dining area was crowded with hundreds of strong, healthy Sea-tizens, formerly known as Under Dwellers, and Tess herself looked robust and happier than she'd been in years. The large pendant draped around her neck indicated her important new role as

Food Source Supervisor, and she was proud to have saved her planet from starvation.

Tess signaled to the preparation area that her table was ready to be served. Three workers carried in the enormous platter of food, and Tess's group began to eat. They cracked the shells of the humanoid-sized shellfish with laser knives, extracting the nourishing meat from the red shells and claws. The hiss of boiling water from the preparation area told the group that more shellfish were being dropped into the cooking vats. There would be plenty for everyone. There always was.

"Can you tell me again why you named this food as you did?" asked a young girl sitting near Tess.

Tess smiled. "I wanted to give the protein food source a name from the planet where it originated," she explained, telling the story again as she had many times since her return from her space journeys. "This came from Earth. In its original form, it was a specimen too small to eat. But once it began ingesting my special slug paste, it began to grow. I researched Earthling data and chose the name of the extinct creature it most resembled—*lobster.* I guess it was my way of honoring a dead planet."

A young male Sea-tizen passed Tess a plate of orange-colored meat. "And what name did you give this food source?" he asked. Tess grinned and wiped her mouth with her napkin. "Ah, yes. I call it *steak.* Don't you think it tastes just marvelous with this lobster?"

All the Sea-tizens nodded their agreement, and as they did, Tess's eyes wandered to the blue waters that surrounded the huge metropolis beneath the ocean. Out there, she knew, the great white sharks patrolled the deep. Of course, most of the magnificent beasts fed in the shallow waters around the Grand Island. Many had made their way through the underwater passages to the inland sea. There was a steady supply of fitapia fish to eat, and a few of the remaining half-starved Lords would regularly plunge into the waters to end their horrid fate.

Tess sighed with contentment. My, how things had changed. Thousands of feet above her, the land was dying. *Yes,* she thought, *the Lords had been right about one thing. Whoever has food has power—that's the law, isn't it?*